William Westall

Birch Dene

A novel. Part 2

William Westall

Birch Dene
A novel. Part 2

ISBN/EAN: 9783337043575

Printed in Europe, USA, Canada, Australia, Japan

Cover: Foto ©Andreas Hilbeck / pixelio.de

More available books at **www.hansebooks.com**

BIRCH DENE.

A Novel.

BY

WILLIAM WESTALL,

AUTHOR OF

"HER TWO MILLIONS," "RED RYVINGTON," "NIGEL FORTESCUE,"
"JOHN BROWN AND LARRY LOHENGRIN," ETC.

IN THREE VOLUMES.

VOL. II.

London:

· WARD AND DOWNEY,

12, YORK STREET, COVENT GARDEN.

1889.

RICHARD CLAY & SONS, LIMITED,
LONDON & BUNGAY.

CONTENTS OF VOLUME II.

BIRCH DENE.

CHAPTER I.

JIM RABBITS.

Tom Cat was by no means a bad fellow, as spinners went in those days. Though he kept a strap and walloped his piecers and creelers now and then, and occasionally threw a clearer or other missile at their heads, he neither tortured them for his pleasure nor spent more than a fourth of his wage in drink. Most of his fellow-workmen, besides getting drunk on Saturdays and Sundays, consumed two or three quarts of beer every working day.

Cat, being a shrewd fellow, was too knowing not to be civil to an apprentice who had been taken in hand by the spinning master. He gave him a first lesson in piecing, and explained the mechanism of the jenny, about which Robin was curious.

"Watch t'others and you'll soon get into it," he said, encouragingly. "But piecing one end doesn't 'mount to much. A chap, to be worth owt, should piece four in a draw; I've known chaps as could piece seven."

After this Cat left Robin to his own devices. At first he felt awkward and bewildered, but the machinery interested him greatly, and as he gained confidence he attempted to piece a thread (technically, an "end").

After many trials he succeeded by a fluke, and fancied himself very clever; but his next attempt ended in disaster. Ends are pieced as the frame (now called mule) draws out, and the further it draws out, the further have the piecers to stretch in order to reach the rollers. Robin, in his eagerness stretching too far, fell head foremost over the front part of the frame, and broke more threads in a second than he was like to piece in a month. Had he not enjoyed the spinning master's favour there would have been hot words—probably blows and a fight; for Robin was a lad of spirit, and knew how to use his fists. But after a big oath, just to relieve his feelings, Cat, laughing heartily, helped Robin to his feet, and stopped the frame to "piece up."

"You mun stan' me a quart for this," he said, "and if you don't do so no more, we'll say nowt about it."

Robin shook his head. He did not possess the price of a gill, much less of a quart.

"Oh, ay—I'd forgotten. Th' Parson has run away wi' all your brass. Never mind! If he's cotched, and your brass is fun', you'll stand then, maybe?"

"With pleasure."

"Good! We'll have it some neet at Lucky Riddles. Fettled?"

"Fettled! What do you mean?"

"Hot, wi' a bit o' nutmeg in't."

"If you like."

"That'll be grand"—(smacking his lips)— "and I'll be a noggin or two o' rum mysel'."

Later in the day, a small boy, with crooked legs and a wizened face, touching Robin on the arm, told him that Jim Rabbits wanted him "in th' cabin," and offered to show him the way.

On this Robin nodded assent, and followed his guide up two or three flights of grimy and greasy stone steps until they came to a door, in the lock of which hung a bunch of keys.

"That's it!" said the boy, and incontinently disappeared.

After knocking at the door—an excess of politeness in the circumstance—and being answered by a request to "Come in," Robin entered "the cabin"—really the spinning master's sanctum, a room about twelve feet square, furnished with a vice, a bench, and a three-legged stool. On the walls hung coils of wire, balls of twine, straps, laces, brushes, cog-wheels, and a miscellaneous collection of odds and ends.

Rabbits had before him a sheet of coarse paper, covered with cabalistic signs in red lead, which bore a remote resemblance to figures, and his swarthy face wore the rapt look of one who has been wrestling with mighty thoughts.

" You said this morning as you could cipher ? " he observed, anxiously.

" I can—a little."

" I wish yo'd cipher for me a bit. I'd make it worth your while. I'm quite at th' far end. I've been trying to work this out for two hours and more, and I'm not a bit forruder."

The spinning master was as weak in the theory of his calling as he was strong in its practice. A calculation bothered him dreadfully, and he had many calculations to make—or rather, many that he ought to have made ; for, save the very simplest, all his work of this description was done for him by the book-keeper, Tommy Nutter, generally called Owd Nutcrackers (in playful allusion to his name, and the fact that his nose and chin promised at no distant time to meet). But Nutcrackers had not the sweetest of tempers. He rendered his help so unwillingly, and at the price of so many pints of beer, that Rabbits was intensely anxious to be independent of him.

At the outset Robin feared that he would not be able to do what was required of him; but when Jim stated the question, and produced a manuscript book, in which rules were given and examples worked out, Robin had no difficulty in solving the problem that had so puzzled his patron—something about the size of a pulley and the speed of a shaft—to the spinning master's great delight.

"One good torn desarves another," he said, "and I'll do you a good torn for this. See if I don't. Tak' th' book and look at it when you've a minute or two to spare, and when I want some more ciphering done, you'll know how to do it. I geet it for th' price of a gallon o' beer from an owd mon as wor on th' boil (on the loose), thinking it might torn out useful, and if I could read it and write like you, I wouldn't give a twopenny damn to call King George my uncle. I might get to be a mayster mysel' then, and mak' my fortune."

Robin hinted that in these circumstances he was rather surprised the spinning master did not learn to read and write.

" Do you think I could ? " (anxiously).

" Why not ? I once heard Mr. Bartlett say that a man with brains may learn anything he likes; and you have brains, or you could not be a spinning master, could you ? "

" Well, there's summat i' that," said Rabbits, thoughtfully. " I know one thing : I've a damned sight more brains than owd Nutcrackers, and he's th' best writer i' these parts, and can figure like a fourteen-day clock. But, then, he larned when he wor young, and I'm thirty come next Michaelmas."

" Still you might try, and I'm sure——"

" But who is there to larn me ? I'd liefer be licked than ax th' book-keeper. Beside, it would cost me hoaf my wage in drink. He can howd as much beer as a brewer's vat, owd Nutcrackers can. There's Bill

Romford ; he's a gradely good scholar too —— But no! It would never do. I durstna."

"Why? Is he like Nutcrackers? Can he hold as much beer as a brewer's vat?"

"Nay, he isn't a supper, isn't Bill. But he's waur—he's a Radical."

This sentiment surprised Robin beyond measure, for he had an idea (gathered, doubtless, from Mr. Bartlett) that Radicals were the salt of the earth.

"How can being a Radical be worse than being a drunkard?" he asked.

"I don't say as it is. But both Ben and Bob's rank Tories. They'd think th' world wor coming to an end if I let a Radical weyver larn me to read. Why, it's not long sin' they bagged a chap for wearing a white hat on a Easter Sunday."

"A white hat! What can there be wrong in that, Mr. Rabbits?"

"Well, I doan't know as there's owt wrong i' th' hat; but wearing one is th' sign of a Radical. Owd Bob said as no mon as respects his mayster, and is loyal to his king, would have such a thing in his house, much less put it on his yed."

"In that case it must be considered loyal to wear a black hat? I wonder why?" asked Robin, with a puzzled look.

"That's more than I can tell you. I don't know much 'bout politics; but I know when I've a good shop, and that's th' main point, Nelson. And I know another thing: if a working mon meddles wi' politics, he's sure to get into a hobble. There's Bill Romford, now. He's been i' two or three hobbles awready, and if he doesn't get hissel' transported afore he's done, it'll chet me. But he's a rare weyver and a fine scholar, and I doan't know a B from a bull's foot. Romford's a better mon than me, Nelson, though he is a Radical."

"If you wouldn't mind," said Robin, hesitatingly, "I think—if you would let me try I could perhaps teach you to read and write. I never did teach anybody, but——"

"Let you try! Ay, will I, and be gradely
fain too, and do my best to larn. But doan't
say nowt. Keep it quiet, whatever you do.
You shall give me my fost lesson o' Sunday.
By gum! willn't Owd Bob stare when he
knows? He'll be saying, as he oft does,
'Here's a letter, Jim, about them spindles,'
or happen about a new roving machine.
'But you cannot read; I'll read it for you.'
And then I'll say, 'You're mista'en, Mester
Robbut—I can read it;' and then I'll let
him see. Willn't he stare! But larn me
to read, Nelson, and I'll do owt for you.
Don't forget Sunday. And now I think
you'd better be going back to your work.
It's welly lighting-up time; I mun be off
mysel', or I shall be having Owd Bob
after me."

Robin went, and as he shut the door
behind him, the spinning master laughed
softly to himself.

"He's a good soort—a gradely good soort,"
he murmured. "He calls me Mester Rabbits,
and he'll learn me to read."

CHAPTER II.

OLD DICK'S ADVICE.

By the time Robin returned to his work lighting-up had begun. It was a slow and tedious process, drawbacks which were not redressed by a brilliant result, for albeit coal-gas as an illuminant was coming into use, it did not yet illuminate Birch Dene. The lamps gave a dim and vacillating light, the smoke thereof blackened the ceiling, and still further fouled the air; and the heat, which before had been oppressive, became almost unbearable.

Several of the lads doffed their shirts; a girl fainted and had to be carried out, the spinners worked with evident effort, the weary and worn-out children could not " keep their ends up," thereby incurring the wrath of their masters, who hurled at them fierce oaths and blood-curdling threats. A spinner at the next pair of wheels to Robin's ran amuck among his piecers with a piece of strapping, and Tom Cat knocked a boy down with his fist.

When the engine stopped (ten minutes after its time) there was a general sense of relief. The hands who lived outside put on their clogs, coats, waistcoats, and caps, wound huge red comforters round their necks (comforters were a great institution at Birch Dene), and hurried off. The apprentices went as they were. Shoeless and half-naked, they picked their way, shivering, through the cindered yard to their wretched quarters. But a bright fire and hot porridge awaited them, and after thirteen hours in the suffocating spinning room, with its jarring noises and monotonous toil, the apprentice-house was a haven of rest and a place of delight. After supper the children recovered their spirits, and began a series of pranks, which ended, as usual, in a row, the appearance of Dick with his horse-whip, and a peremptory dismissal to bed.

But he made an exception in Robin's favour.

"You can sit by th' fireside, and go to bed when you like," he said. "You're not like t'others; you're a young mon, and a schollard."

By calling him a "young mon" Dick meant not merely that Robin was a well-grown lad who could read and write, but that he ranked in popular estimation as something very different from a common apprentice or ordinary factory hand. Mr. Nutter had been heard to say that Nelson's handwriting was almost as good as his own, and that he had read more books than the two Ruberrys had ever seen. Jim Rabbits, on his part, had confided to the carding-master his belief that Nelson had more wit in his little finger than many up-grown folk carried in their heads.

This expression of opinion being repeated and passed on with additions, it came to pass that before Robin had been at Birch Dene a week he was regarded as a sort of Admiral Crichton—or would have been had the Birch

Dene folks ever heard of that portentous genius—and they wondered greatly who he was, and how he had become the master of so many accomplishments and so much knowledge.

Robin gladly accepted Dick's invitation to take a seat by the fireside. He was in no hurry to leave its friendly warmth for that greasy and, if the truth must be told, rather too lively bed of his in the garret.

"You'd better ha' stopped in London, I think," observed Dick, as he lighted his pipe with a coal from the fire.

"I wish I had," answered Robin, with a rueful glance at his grimy trousers and bare feet.

"If it's a fair question, I'd like to know what med you come; and there's more than me as would like to know."

On this Robin told briefly, pretty much as he told Major Dene, what had happened to him since Mr. Bartlett's death.

Dick smoked reflectively, as if the narrative contained matter for thought, then smiled

complacently, as if he had hit upon a very
original idea.

"That's it," he said, removing his pipe
from his mouth—"that's it. I thowt there
was summat out of th' common. You've
lived among books; that accounts for your
being such a schollard, and knowing so much
about 'em. But I'll tell you what—that
whaten-you-caw-him—Weevil, is a damned
rogue!"

Robin nodded assent.

"He's nowt else. He is a damned rogue!
If ever he comes to Birch Dene he'll get his
shins punched. I can promise him that. He
told you a pack o' lies to get rid of you, and
keep th' owd fellow's brass for hissel'. Are
you sure, now, as Bartlett wasn't your
fayther?"

"Certainly," said Robin, half amused, half
indignant. "How could he be? My name is
Nelson; his was Bartlett."

"That's nowt," returned Dick, with a knowing smile—"nowt at all. Why, there's scores
o' childer in these parts as isn't called after

their faythers, and mony a one as doesn't know who their faythers is. Who was your mother ? "

" My mother died when I was very young," said Robin, evasively. He had a decided objection to discussing his mother with Old Dick.

" Well, it's nowt to me ; but I can happen see as far into a stone wall as onybody else. Howsomever, there's one thing clear—you're a 'prentice, bun' till twenty-one. It is a gradely hard case, I will say that—and you'll happen have thowts o' running away. But I don't think I would if I wor you. You'd ten to one get catched and put i' prison, and you wouldn't like that ; and runaway 'prentices mostly does get catched, either dead or alive."

" Dead or alive ! What do you mean ? "

" Only as they sometimes dee," said Dick, composedly. " Last winter two lads run away from here—one of th' spinners had been hiding 'em a bit moor than usual. Well, they were fun' th' week after on th' moors, frozen to death, and their een pyked out by crows. I don't say as owt o' that sort would happen to you. All th' same, I'd stop where you are, if I wor you. It's not as if you wor a common 'prentice. You are a fine schollard and a young mon, and they're sure to find you summut better to do than piecing. Tak' care as you keep in wi' Owd Bob, that's all."

"Why with him more than Mr. Ruberry?" asked Robin, who could not yet bring himself to speak of his employers in the free-and-easy style adopted by Dick and the others.

"Because he's th' cock o' this here midden. Whatever he wants is done, whatever he doesn't want isn't done. Th' hands says as Ben's bark is waur than his bite, and as Bob's bite is waur than his bark. If Ben bags a chap, he'll shop him ageean th' week after; but if Bob bags a chap, he mut as weel whistle jigs to a milestone as ax on ageean. Bob's most terrible hot again th' Parson. He wor in here this afternoon. You'll have yerd as his clothes has been fun'."

"No, I haven't. Where? Have any of mine been found?" exclaimed Robin, eagerly.

"They were fun' in a field about a mile off, on th' Manchester road—his owd things, nowt else. He doffed his own and donned yours, and then made off with th' portmantle. But they're cock-sure to catch him. Th' portmantle 'll be his ruin. He'd ha' shown some sense if he had left that in th' field too. He'll be trying to pop summat, and then he'll get dropped on. And a bonny hobble he'll be in! They say as Owd Bob means to make a hanging job on it."

"For stealing my clothes?"

"For nowt else. You surely don't think as they'd scrag a slip of a lad for running away! They haven't getten to that yet. Not as I think Owd Bob would have owt ageean it. He'd hang a runaway 'prentice as soon as look, if he could have his way."

Robin had no reason to bear the Parson good will. The theft of his clothes was both mean and cruel, and if he met Blincoe, the latter would be very likely to pass a bad quarter of an hour. But hanging him would be too horrible; and for the hundredth time there arose before Robin's mental vision the ghastly scene at the Old Bailey; the terrible words of the judge rang once more in his ears; he saw his mother sink dying in the dock, and, closing his eyes, visibly shuddered.

"You're cowd," said Dick. "Draw a bit nearer to th' fire. I'll stor it up a bit. Them clothes isn't warm enough for you out o' th' factory. I mun see if I cannot get summat warmer for you by Sunday, and fit you up wi' stockings and a pair o' shoon. And now, if you're not in a horry to go to bed, you'd happen not mind reading a bit for Betty and me—hoo'll be here in a minute. It isn't oft as we getten onybody to read to us. Jabez o' Jenny's lass can do a bit, but hoo gets o'er no ground—has to spell every second word, and then hoo doesn't know what they mean. I've a bit of a book there, in th' nook, as I bowt ov a hawker for fourpence and a pint o' beer. He said as it wor gradely good reading, and there's an uncommon nice cut on th' back."

As Dick spoke he went to a corner cupboard, and returned with his " bit of a book," which proved to be a pamphlet, giving a full, true, and particular account of an exceptionally brutal murder, and the murderer's last dying speech and confession. The " uncommon nice cut" was a ghastly engraving of a man hanging—supposed to be the murderer—Jack Ketch pulling at his legs, and a devil in the background, presumably waiting to receive his soul.

" A gradely good 'un, isn't it ? " said the old man, admiringly. " But I never knew afore as th' owd lad had a gimlet at th' end of his tail. I reckon he makes it red hot, and uses it to bore hoyles in 'em when he gets 'em there. Come on, Betty "—(shouting)—" Nelson is going to read this book as I bowt fro' th' hawker ! "

Robin would much rather have gone to bed, but, not liking to disoblige his host and hostess, especially after the former's fatherly advice, he complied with Dick's wish, and read the pamphlet from beginning to end, to the worthy couple's great delight, which, as also their admiration of his cleverness, was warmly expressed.

"What I like about his reading," observed Betty, "is as he stops at nowt, nayther stutters nor stammers, but goes straight on, as if he wor telling it all out of his own yed."

"Thou art reyt, lass, he does," added her husband, sympathetically. "Th' words comes out of his mouth like watter out of a spout on a rainy day. We'll have some o' th' chaps in next time as he reads, and I'll be twopence to'ard another book if onybody else will."

After this all went to bed, and so ended Robin's second day at Birch Dene—a memorable day in his life's history—a day which he was not likely ever to forget. The expectations raised by that rascal, Moses Weevil, had been rudely and finally dispelled. Robin had learned beyond a doubt that, call himself what he might, he was nothing better than a common parish apprentice, bound to serve the brothers Ruberry for three years at the munificent salary of a shilling a week. On the other hand, he was not so badly off as some of his companions; the place and, above all, the machinery interested him; he felt a desire to understand it, and to know more of the properties and nature of steam, which seemed to him as wonderful and mysterious as the imprisoned genii he had read about in *The Arabian Nights*. Even though his clothes and his money had not been stolen, he would probably have thought twice before attempting to carry out his project of escape, and to attempt it in existing circumstances would be the height of folly.

For the moment, moreover, his chief concern was the recovery of his lost belongings. Should he ever get them back? he was continually asking himself. To be without a change of garments; to have neither comb nor brush, nor possess a clean shirt; to be compelled, out of the factory as well as in it, to wear the miserable garments given him by his masters—all this was more than an inconvenience, it was a degradation. He felt

like somebody else—could hardly believe that
but a few weeks previously he was a happy
youth, with fair prospects and kind friends.

When Robin awoke next morning, he
thought at first that it was all a hideous
dream; but the hoarse clang of the factory
bell, the cries of his comrades, and the voice
of Old Dick shouting that if they did not
look sharp he would be at them with his
whip, quickly dispelled the illusion, and
tumbling out of his bunk, he slipped on his
trousers, and was one of the first down-stairs.
Dick would probably have let him stay in
bed a little longer, but he had made up his
mind to conform to the rules, and show that
what others could do he could do. One indulgence, however, he did crave and obtain;
he prevailed on Betty to give him a towel
and let him wash in the kitchen, instead of
doing his ablutions at the pump, and strug-
gling for "a dry wipe" with a corner of the
piece of coarse sheeting used for that purpose
by his fellow apprentices. Then he took a
hunch of bread and went to his work.

The day passed pretty much as the previous day had passed. Robin contrived to piece about a dozen ends without tumbling over the frame, and was warmly commended by Tom Cat for his success. In the afternoon he spent an hour with the spinning master in his cabin, doing calculations, and giving him a preliminary reading lesson. Fired with zeal for knowledge, Rabbits was too impatient to wait until Sunday; he wanted "summat to larn" in the meanwhile; and during the remainder of the day he might occasionally be seen taking from his waistcoat-pocket and furtively consulting the "bit o' papper" whereon Robin had inscribed, in bold characters, the letters of the alphabet.

CHAPTER III.

IF nothing particular happened on the third day of Robin's sojourn at Birch Dene, a good deal happened on the fourth. Shortly after breakfast time, as he was reaching over to piece an end, the machinery came to a dead stop.

"Hello!" shouted Tom Cat. "What's up, I wonder? I expect it's them spor-wheels in th' bottom room. I yerd Jim say as they worn't running true. If they're smashed we shall have to lake [play] a week, and if we do my children will have to go short o' porridge. But it's happen summat wrong with th' engin'."

A minute later the spinning master, popping his head in at the door, confirmed Cat's conjecture. The crank shaft of the engine had heated, but the stoppage was not expected to last more than half an hour.

Robin had not the most remote idea what a crank shaft was, or why its heating should render necessary a stoppage of all the machinery, and in his thirst for knowledge he plied Tom Cat with more questions than that worthy could satisfactorily answer.

"Go and see for yoursel," said Tom, at last, rather impatiently. "They'll let you look. Go through No. 2, and down th' steps into the boiler-house—that's th' nearest road."

Robin acted on this suggestion at once. No. 2 was the room below No. 3 (the one in which he worked).

As he opened the door he heard shouts of laughter and cries of pain.

A spinner, known as Black Jack, was whiling away his enforced leisure by torturing one of the apprentices, or, as he would have said, having a "bit o' sport." A poor boy, not more than ten years old, had been forced to take off his clothes, and Jack was now trying to make him sit on a hot steam-pipe. The child struggled and begged for mercy, but he was answered only by jeers and laughter; and as his body touched the burning iron, he screamed and writhed in agony, greatly, as it seemed, to the amusement of the spinners, piecers, and others who were looking on.

This was more than Robin could stand, and without giving a thought to the consequences, he ran forward, pushed Black Jack aside, and lifted the child from the pipe, a proceeding which was followed by exclamations of surprise from the spectators, and a howl of rage from the principal actor.

"What the hell!" he shouted. . . . "If thou doesn't pyke off this minute, I'll clap thee on th' pipe too, thou damned Cockney counter-jumper. Come, be off, now!"

And Black Jack made as if he would again lay hands on his victim.

"You shall not touch this child," said Robin, as he stood between them, pale and in a tremor of excitement, yet with undaunted mien.

"Who's going to stop me? Not a hatter-cropper [spider] like thee! But if thou'll stan' thy ground I'll give thee what for afore I set Little Jimmy on ageean. What says thou?"

"I wouldn't if I was you," whispered a friendly piecer; "he's a deal stronger than you."

This was quite true. Black Jack (so called because of his swarthy, ill-favoured face), though short of stature, was broad of chest, and his arms, by reason of his occupation, were as strong as sledge hammers.

But Robin did not flinch.

"You may do what you like," he said, quietly; "but I shall stay here until you promise to let the boy alone, and while I stay you shall not lay a hand on him."

"Thou wants sore bones then, and thou shall have 'em. Come on!"

And by way of showing that he meant what he said, Black Jack rolled up his shirt-sleeves and spat fiercely into his hands—the usual preliminary to battle. Then, drawing a few steps backwards, he paused, as if half expecting that Robin, overawed by his resolute attitude, might yield him the honours of victory without striking a blow.

On this some of the others began to laugh.

"Thou dare not tackle him, Jack," said one.

"He'll be too mony for thee, owd mon," shouted another.

These taunts stirred Jack to immediate action.

Lowering his arms, he made a rush at his opponent, as if he would bear him down by sheer strength. This rather surprised Robin, and if Jack had been armed with his clogs it might have fared ill with the lad, for he had no experience of Lancashire fighting. But, being barefooted, the spinner could make no effectual use of his feet, and being no boxer, he meant to grip Robin by the waist, throw him down, and then "punch his head." This design Robin defeated by a very simple manœuvre. As Jack made his rush, he gave him a blow with "his left"

between the eyes, delivered straight from the
shoulder, and the spinner went down like a
felled ox.

"Jump on him and finish him! Get on
to him and throttle him! Look sharp, or
he'll be up ageean!" shouted the now excited
onlookers, who could not for the life of them
understand why Robin did not follow up his
advantage.

But Robin, who had no idea of hitting a
man when he was down, waited quietly until
the spinner got up.

"Thou had better give in," said one of his
friends. "Another crack like that theer, and
thou'll be that faa [ugly] as thy own wife
willn't know thee."

"Not I," growled Jack, savagely. "I
haven't begun yet." And with that he
lowered his head and went at Robin like a
bull charging.

The next moment Jack's head was in
"chancery."

In vain he struggled to free himself. It
is no easy thing to get out of "chancery"

at any time, and when your opponent has a firm grip of your neck, and is hammering away at your face, the feat is well-nigh impossible, and Robin, who by this time was in a decidedly berserker frame of mind, showed no mercy, showering his blows like rain, and sticking to his man like grim death.

Like James FitzJames and Roderick Dhu, they tug and strain, and at length, their feet slipping on the greasy floor, down they go, Robin uppermost, and still holding on.

And then the shouts suddenly cease, and an ominous whisper passes from mouth to mouth.

"I give in. Leave loose! Let me get up!" says Black Jack, in a hoarse gurgle. "It's Owd Bob!"

Robin loosed his hold, and both combatants scrambled to their feet.

Robert Ruberry was at the door, looking sternly on, and the spectators of the fight were slinking away one by one, or, as they would have said, "pyking off."

"What!" he exclaimed, "cannot the engine

stop a few minutes but you must be fighting?
The only way with you fellows is to keep
your noses to the grindstone. Who are the
fighters? Nelson and Black Jack! Why,
Nelson, I thought you called yourself a
scholar, and considered yourself a bit of a
gentleman! I did not know that your
scholarship included a knowledge of up-and-
down fighting. What were you fighting
for?—a quart of beer? Or was it merely
to decide which of you is the better
man?"

"Neither one nor the other, Mr. Robert,"
answered Robin, indignantly; and then he
told what had happened, emphasizing his
narrative by pointing to the naked child,
who was cowering behind him.

"Oh, that was it, was it! Well, I think
you did quite right, Nelson. Apprentices
cost money; we cannot afford to have 'em
frizzled on hot steam-pipes. If that lad had
been injured and laid up, it might have run
us into a loss of four or five pounds, one way
and another. Strap 'em if you like, but we'll

have no burning. What had he been doing?
—Little Jimmy I mean."

" I don't know as he had been doing owt.
It was nobbut a bit o' sport," said Jack,
sullenly, as he wiped his bleeding face with
a piece of cotton waste.

" Sport ! Well, sport with your own
children next time. You can stick them on
the steam-pipe as much as you like. But
I'll have no sporting with our apprentices.
Why, man, what a face you have got ! It
will be as black as my hat soon. Your own
wife won't know you."

" Just what I said just now," observed one
of the fellows who had stood his ground.
" He's faaer than ever. I cannot tell what
he wor doing to let a bit of a lad peyl him
in that way."

" A bit of a lad ! " growled Jack. " He'd
lick thee ony end up, and thou caws thysel'
an up-grown fellow ! He fights like him
as he's called after—Lord Nelson—crashed
me down afore I knew where I wor', by
gum !"

"Come! No more of this! All of you to
your places; the engine is setting on again,"
cried Robert Ruberry, impatiently. "And
you, Nelson, go to your own room. How
came you here?"

Robin told him.

"So you are both curious and combative.
But take care you are not too combative. If
Jack had had his clogs on, you might have
got a good deal the worst of it. But you
cannot be too curious about owt as it concerns
you to know. Learn all you can, and study
your master's interest, and you may become a
valuable servant."

Coming from Robert Ruberry this was a
gracious saying; but Robin returned to his
work with the conviction that the younger
brother was a tyrannical old curmudgeon,
yet fully satisfied with what he had done,
and proud of his victory over Black Jack.
The news of it reached No. 3 before him,
and as he entered the room he was received
with a cheer. Tom Cat congratulated him
warmly.

"You sarved him weel reyt," he said. "I don't hold wi' putting childer on hot steam pipes. But I've seen it done, and it is done. And, what's more, I've seen a lad hoisted up to a hook by his hands, wi' weights fastened to his feet, and then hided wi' a piece of thick belting till he lost his senses. I don't hold with that nayther. But what caps me is how you managed to best Black Jack. If he is not long, he's strong, and though you're taller, you are nowt like as heavy. You're a good plucked 'un, and sharp wi' your neaves (fists), that mun be it. They sayen as you knocked him down like winking."

Besides congratulations, Robin's victory made him the popular hero of the hour, and brought him a nickname. The apprentices swore by him, and before nightfall he was dubbed, by general consent, "Little Lord Nelson," and the sobriquet, sometimes shortened to "Little Lord," or "Lord Nelson" simply, according to the fancy of the speaker, stuck to Robin until he found his own name.

Later in the day, while he was watching Tom Cat tighten a driving strap, the wizen-faced lad who had summoned him to the spinning master's cabin touched him on the arm, in the same mysterious way as before, and whispered that he was "wanted in th' counting-house."

Robin's first idea was that the brothers were going to call him over the coals for thrashing Black Jack; but on consideration he saw that this was hardly likely, as, on the whole, "Owd Bob" had commended him, although grudgingly and ungraciously. However, he would soon see.

In the passage leading to the counting-house were several of the hands, among them Old Dick, obviously in an intensely expectant state of mind.

"Get you in," said Dick, "and yo'll see summat as you want to see."

Inside there was quite a crowd — the brothers Ruberry, Jim Rabbits, Nutter, two strangers whom Robin rightly conjectured to be constables, and a youth, whom he at once knew to be the Parson, though he had never seen him before. On the floor lay his missing valise.

All the wrath that Robin had been nursing against Blincoe evaporated at the sight of him. Never had he seen a more abject specimen of humanity. Blincoe was under-sized and dreadfully knock-kneed; his arms were disproportionately long; his short-cropped hair made visible several ugly scars; he had a furtive, hang-dog look, and his ill-favoured face was covered with eruptions. Altogether, a most wretched-looking creature—not natur-ally, but made so by cruel usage and a life of enforced servitude and excessive toil. Had he been born under a happier star, kindly treated, and carefully trained, he might have been as healthy, as high-spirited, and as well-favoured as Robin himself. Yet probably not one of the men present experienced even a passing sense of pity for the manacled victim of social oppression and unrighteous laws who stood trembling before them. They saw in him only a runaway and a thief, fully deserving of all the punishment which his crimes might entail and justice (!) inflict.

"Is this your property, Nelson?" asked Robert Ruberry, pointing to the valise.

"Yes, sir," answered Robin, after examining the contents; "and very few of my things seem to be missing."

"You can swear to them?"

"Certainly!"

"And the clothes Blincoe has on, are they also yours?"

Robin had no doubt of it, but in order to make quite sure, he examined them carefully, and then gave the same answer as before.

"Well, we shall want you to give your evidence to-morrow. Were you ever in a court of justice?"

"Yes, sir," said Robin, with a strange look.

"Then there's no occasion for me to say owt. You know all about it. Let's see, what time do the justices meet?"—(to one of the constables).

"Half-past ten."

"You will have to start a bit before ten then. Be ready at half-past nine, Nelson. Either my brother or I will go with you. It will be a very simple affair. You will have little more to do than swear to your things and be bound over to prosecute."

"Yes, sir. But may I have some of my things? If not, I shall find it rather difficult to be more ready than I am at present."

"I see no objection. You can swear to them just as well whether they are in your bag or on your back. What do you think, Jenkinson?"

"Oh, ay; th' thing belongs to him. Let him have what he wants. But we must tak' th' portmantle and what there is beside. Th' portmantle's worth a sovereign, let alone owt else; and that is enough to cook his goose" (indicating Blincoe with a jerk of his thumb). "But what are you going to do wi' him till morning?"

"I thought of locking him up in th' old warehouse. He will not get out, I'll warrant him, and old Dick can give him a bit of supper."

"Ay, I dare say that'll do; and we'll be here first thing in th' morning to look after him."

And so the colloquy came to an end. The constables took their prisoner to the old warehouse, and Robin went out with Jim Rabbits, who told how Blincoe had been "dropped on." At the outset he had a stroke of luck. After changing his working clothes for a suit of Robin's he took to the high road, and fell in with a carrier bound from Rochdale to Manchester, who agreed to carry him and his bag to the latter place for a shilling and a pint of beer. He thus got away from Birch Dene without being seen, or leaving any clue as to the direction he had taken.

"If it had not been for that cart," said the spinning master, "he'd ha' been catched afore he'd been gone two hours."

At Manchester Blincoe put up at a small hostelry in Deansgate, his purpose being to travel to London by waggon. But as after settling his score at the inn he would not have nearly enough to pay his fare and other expenses, it was necessary for him to raise the wind either by pawning or selling some of Robin's property. Fearing to enter a "pop-shop," lest it might lead to his detection, and desiring to keep the clothes for his own use, so that he might, as he put it to himself, "travel respectable," he decided, after long consideration, to dispose of the books, and, by way of a beginning, took the *Shakespeare* and the *Paradise Lost* to a second-hand book-seller near the Collegiate Church steps.

This proceeding proved the Parson's ruin, or, as Jim Rabbits expressively remarked, "it did for him."

The bookseller, either struck by something in Blincoe's manner, or the fact of the *Paradise Lost* being a scarce edition, asked Blincoe how he had come by the books.

"I bought them in London," said Blincoe, boldly.

As it happened, this was not a bad shot,

the inscription on the fly-leaf being dated at
London.

"Lately?"

"Two years since."

A very bad shot, for the inscription pur-
ported to have been written only a few
months previously, and the bookseller began
to smell a rat.

"This copy of *Paradise Lost* seems to be
rather a valuable book. What do you ask
for it?"

"It was not lost, I tell you; I bought
it. What will you give me for it and that
other?"

On this the bookseller, feeling sure that the
books had not been honestly come by, said
that he should detain them and communicate
with the police. After an angry but useless
protest against this proceeding, Blincoe made
off as fast as his shambling legs could carry
him. But the bookseller caused him to be
watched, and a few hours later he was in
custody.

"If he'd been a schollard," observed the

spinning master, sententiously, " he'd ha' had more sense than to try to sell a book wi' th' owner's name written inside. I tell you what it is, Nelson; whether a chap's a rogue or an honest mon, or just as it happens, sometimes a bit of one, sometimes a bit of t'other, like the generality of folk, he's not up to much if he doesn't know how to read and write. Come into th' cabin a minute or two, and hear me say my A B, *ab*, and look at these pothooks as I made last neet."

CHAPTER IV.

THE OLD WAREHOUSE.

THE old warehouse was an isolated one-storeyed building, dimly lighted from the roof, with a door wide enough to admit a loaded truck. The walls streamed with moisture, and the flagged floor was thick with grease. The warehouse contained a pair of beam weigh scales, sundry bales of cotton, bags of waste, casks of oil, and barrels of tallow. Besides being a happy hunting-ground for rats, it had the reputation of being haunted by the ghost of an overlooker, who, in a fit of delirium tremens, had hung himself behind the door with a bale rope.

It was to this place that Blincoe, after being made to doff Robin's clothes and put on his own, was conducted by the constables.

The wretched lad, who stood in mortal terror of ghosts and rats, besought them to put him somewhere else.

"For God's sake, don't leave me here all by mysel'!" he cried, piteously. "Anywhere but here—anywhere but here. I'll not try to get out. . . . For God's sake——"

But the constables had their orders, and as he resisted strenuously, they dragged him in by main force; and cursing him for his stupidity, threw him on a heap of waste, and left him to make the best of it.

So long as it was not quite dark, and he could hear the hum of machinery in the mill, Blincoe did not despair, but when the last glimmer of light died out, and the patter of departing feet told him that the people were going home, and that in a few minutes he would be utterly alone, he groped his way to the door, and screamed wildly for mercy and help. Yet neither mercy nor help came, and after a while he lay down again on the pile of waste. The darkness was now absolute; he could not see his uplifted hand, and

the stillness was broken only by the squeaking
of the rats as they tumbled from the cotton
bales and raced over the floor.

Blincoe had heard terrible stories of rats
setting on people in lonely places, flying at
their throats, and biting them to death, and
when one of the creatures brushed against his
leg, and another ran over his face, he jumped
to his feet with a yell. In imagination he
saw them swarming about him in thousands.

How can he defend himself? Happy
thought, the scales! And the next moment
he is frantically hurling all the weights he
can lay hands on at his invisible foes. This
seems to settle them; the squeakings cease,
and he can breathe once more. But he knows
not how long the respite may endure, and not
daring either to lie down or sit, he stands up,
grasping the while one of the weigh scale
chains, and thinking fearfully of the long
hours that must pass before he can hope to
be released.

How many hours? The big factory clock
strikes eight. It will not be light till seven

next morning. Eleven hours—eleven mortal hours! An eternity! Would morning ever come? And the darkness! And the rats! . . .

And—and—the rats had put it out of his mind; but now he remembers and shudders—Ned Dawson's spirit! He is within a yard or two of the very spot where Ned hanged himself. Tom o' Jeffs and Old Dick cut the body down, and he has heard them tell that the face was black and the tongue sticking out, and that the miserable man, rueing the deed at the last moment, tore his throat almost to pieces in his desperate efforts to undo the rope. The sight, they said, was terrifying.

No wonder that Ned's spirit haunts the old warehouse!

Blincoe's blood runs cold; his teeth rattle in his head; he can feel the sweat stream down his face, and hear it as it falls in heavy drops on the floor. . . .

God be thanked! A gleam of light! Blincoe shouts with joy. That yellow moonbeam, shining through the windows, is like water in a thirsty land. Will it go on shining all night? Rats? Not one to be seen. Yet they are running about all the same, and, by way of preparing for the next encounter, he replaces the weights, and possesses himself of a brush-handle. Then, gaining courage, he begins to pace to and fro, for the place is damp and cold, and himself thinly clad.

But what is that hanging from a beam over the door? A hideous thing, with a rope round its neck, a drooping head, and contorted limbs. A corpse, or Ned Dawson's ghost?

Blincoe feels his hair bristle on his head, his knees bend under him, and with a groan of terror he falls on the floor in a dead faint.

A few minutes later the door opens, and in come Robin and Dick, the one carrying a lantern, the other a loaf of bread.

"Where is he?" says Dick.

"There," says Robin, holding up the lantern, and going towards the spot where Blincoe lies prone.

"Asleep! It's a queer place to fa' asleep in. I'd ha' chosen a softer place if I'd been him. There's plenty o' sacks and things about.

Get up, mon! We've brought thee thy supper"—(stirring the prostrate youth with his foot).

"He's not asleep; he's dead!" exclaims Robin, starting back in affright.

"Dead! Not him. Howd th' lantern here —o'er. his face. No, he's none dead. He's swooned on a hempty belly—that's what it is. We mun get some o' this porridge into him. Brun a bit o' brown papper, Nelson, and stick it under his nose."

Robin tears a piece from the wrapper of a cotton sample, lights it at the lantern, and holds it before Blincoe's face; whereupon the lad, sighing deeply, opens his eyes and looks wildly round.

"Where am I?" he murmurs.

"In th' owd warehouse, to be sure; and we've brought thee thy supper. Get up, mon, and knock some o' this porridge into thee. Thou'rt hungered."

"But the corpse—Ned Dawson's spirit? It nearly frightened me to death. And—and —it's there yet, my God!—there yet!"—

(shuddering, and putting his hands before his face).

"Where—where?" exclaimed Dick.

"Over the door."

"Well, I'll be dam—— I mean God help us! Another chap gone and hanged hissel'! Whatever mun we do?" And Dick, looking as scared as Blincoe himself, leans, limp and helpless, against the nearest cotton bale.

"Nothing of the sort," says Robin, laughing, for being keener-sighted than Dick, and less bewildered than Blincoe, he has already detected the true character of the apparition. "Nothing of the sort—it's only a sack."

"Well, I'll be —— I do believe you're reyt. Bithmen, it's nowt else. Why, Parson, what a goamless beggar thou mun be to let a hempty sack flay [frighten] thee into a fit! Onybody can see what it is wi' hoaf an ee."

And with that Dick went boldly up to the sack and shook it.

"It looks most terrible like a corpse, though, doesn't it?" said Blincoe, sheepishly, as, with Robin's help, he rose to his feet.

"Not it," responded Dick, contemptuously. "Thou looks a good deal more like one thysel'. Here, knock this porridge into thee; it'll give thee corridge."

Blincoe sat down on a bag of waste and did as he was told, declaring thereafter that he felt decidedly better. But when his visitors made as if they would leave, he begged pitifully that he might go with them.

"There's thousands of rats," he pleaded; "you know there is. Only a bit sin' they were running all over me. And Ned Dawson's spirit; it's welly sure to come when th' clock strikes twelve. Let me go with you, Dick, and sleep in a coffin. I willn't run away. Tie my legs and arms—do owt you like; but for God's sake don't leave me here all night by mysel'."

Dick shook his head.

"It connot be allowed on," he said, gravely —"it connot be allowed on. Owd Bob has gan his orders, and I darn't go ageean 'em."

"Oh, Dick, do let me go with you. Owd Bob will never know. You can bring me back before daylight. If you leave me I shall either die or lose my senses—I know I shall."

"Nay, nay, it connot be allowed on. Thou'll none lose thy senses, not thou—what bit thou has. Lie thee down and go asleep; nowt'll hurt thee."

"The rats will eat me up. There they are, squeaking again! Don't you hear them?"

"Would you be afraid if somebody were to stay with you?" asked Robin, who had listened to the conversation with deep interest.

"No; I should not be lonesome then. And it is the loneliness as terrifies me so—more than the rats. But who will stay with me?"

"I will."

"You! Why, I stole all your money and took all your clothes!"

"Never mind that. I will stay with him, Dick. He evidently is not fit to be left alone. See how he trembles, and his face is as white as a sheet."

"Are yo' i' gradely arnest?"

"Certainly."

"Well, if you are, I think it can be allowed

on. Owd Bob said as th' Parson wor to be locked up here all neet; but he didn't say as nobody wor to be locked up wi' him. Ay, stop if you will. And I'll tell you what I'll do: I'll fot some blankets for you—it's a cowdish neet; and what's more, I'll bring Scamp. You'll be aw reyt then. He fears naythur rattens nor devil; and it is my belief as he'd fly at Ned Dawson's spirit if he wor to see it—as soon as look. He could ne'er abide him when he wor wiek."

On this idea Dick acted forthwith. In a few minutes he was back with a bundle of blankets and a vicious-looking black and tan terrier.

"Theyre," he said. "There's blankets to keep you warm, and a tyke to tak' care on you. I'll let you out at five o'clock, Nelson, afore onybody's stirring, and then nobody 'ull know nowt. Good-neet to you."

"It is gradely good of you to do me this kindness, Nelson, after the way I behaved to you," said Blincoe, when the old man was gone. "I don't deserve it."

"Well, it was not very nice of you to take my things. But I know how much you have suffered; and you were so terribly frightened that it seemed cruel to leave you in this place all by yourself, so I said I would stay with you, and as I have got all my things back, it does not matter, you know; and I always feel sorry for anybody who is in trouble."

"If you'll believe me, Nelson, if you'll believe me, I didn't mean you any ill when I took your things. I was that hot on getting away as I could think about nowt else. Over my head, within reach of my hand, was clothes and money. I felt sure as if I had them I could get back to London—and I could have done if I hadn't tried to sell them books"—(sighing). . . . "If you only knew, Nelson. But I hope you never will know. It isn't the rough lodgings and coarse food; it isn't the blows and cursings—a chap gets used to them. It is the long, weary hours—piece, piece, piece, week after week, year after year, all day long; no hope, no rest, no change, nowt but piecing ends—factory and bed, bed and factory—nobody to care for you, nobody to say a kind word to you. Eight years I have had of it, and nearly four yet to come! I think I'd liefer die, Nelson."

And then the lad told Robin his miserable story; how he remembered, though dimly, his home and his father and mother. He thought his father must have been a prosperous trades- man in the West-end of London; for they had a good house and himself a nurse, and he used often to be taken for a drive in the country. And then the father died, and they went to a smaller house—where, he could not tell. After that more trouble. His mother fell into bad health, and after a long illness she, too, died. Then strange men came, and Blincoe was taken to St. Pancras Workhouse. He did not complain of his treatment there. It was not, perhaps, all that could be desired; he did not much like it at the time, but it was out of all comparison better than the treatment he had received since, either at Lowdham Mills or Birch Dene. He wished he was back, how he wished he was back! He was sent away in a batch of fifty or sixty boys and girls, all of whom, under the belief, industriously fostered by the beadles, that they would be handsomely treated, and made into ladies and gentlemen, went more than willingly. Within a twelvemonth of their arrival at Lowdham, averred Blincoe, fully one-half were under the sod, and the others, half-starved, continually beaten, and cruelly over-worked, were dragging on a miserable existence, and almost more dead than alive.

And Blincoe's story was probably in no wise exaggerated. As may be seen by reference to the personal narratives of some of the victims who survived, and to Parliamentary Blue Books of the period, his sufferings were far from being exceptional. Factory masters at that time were wont to boast that they used up so many children a year, and every year thousands perished of overwork and ill-usage.

Blincoe did not seem to care much what became of him. He could not well be worse off in prison than he had been at Lowdham Mill and Birch Dene; he would at least have a rest; and, if they hanged him, the rest would know no wakening—that was all. Though he did not put his philosophy into words, he had come to the conclusion that, so far as concerned himself, life was not worth living—and no wonder.

After they had ended their talk, the two lads fell asleep, and when Dick came to rouse them in the morning, Scamp was contemplating with extreme satisfaction half a dozen rats which he had killed during the night.

CHAPTER V.

BEFORE THE BENCH.

AFTER breakfast Robin "knocked off" work and put on his Sunday clothes. How pleasant to discard, though only for a few hours, his greasy garments, enjoy the luxury of a clean shirt—revel in the consciousness that he was himself again ! He felt inches taller, and old Betty paid him the compliment of admiring glances and flattering words.

"It becomes you gradely weel, that suit does," she said, putting her hands on her hips and eyeing him critically. They don't mak' clothes like them theer down here, nor legs nayther. Most on 'em is ayther knock-kneed or bow-legged, or else their coaves is like Tom Oddy's crutch—thick at th' sma' end. And your face has a colour, too, and you've a back as straight as a picking-rod. It is much if you'll have ayther colour, or a straight back, or straight legs after you've been a twelvemonth in th' factory. You'd mak' a rare sodger, after you've thickened a bit, and getten a year or two owder. I'd a brother a sodger, but that's a long while sin', and he wor killed, poor lad, at Bunker's Hill. I wor gradely sorry at th' time, but I've thowt sin' as it wor happen a good job. He's missed a deal of trouble."

Robin, who always took an interest in soldiers, encouraged Betty to go on talking about her brother, and the subject was far from exhausted when Jim Rabbits came in and told him that he was to go with Mr. Ruberry in the gig to Toppleton, while Blincoe, under the escort of the two constables, was to proceed thither on foot.

Robin owed this honour to " Owd Bob."

" Better take him with you, and then you will be sure of him," said the younger brother. " These apprentices are not to be trusted, and you would look small if your principal witness wasn't to turn up."

" Very well. He shall go in the gig, though he is but an apprentice. However, he has a decent suit of clothes, and will look respectable. Do you think we should have 'Torney Bruff?"

"No! Why should we throw thirteen-and-fourpence away? And that is what he'd charge, at the very least. Those lawyers haven't a bit of conscience. If Blincoe had anybody to speak for him it would be different. But he hasn't. State the case yourself. All you have to say is what he is charged with, and call on Nelson to tell his tale. Th' magistrate will commit him, of course—they can do nowt else; and then we must get th' Crown to prosecute. It's a capital felony."

"As you seem to know so much about it, hadn't you better go yourself?" said Benjamin, rather tartly; for although he generally did his brother's bidding without demur, he was occasionally provoked to rebellion.

"No; this sort of thing is more in your line than mine. Besides, I never leave th' ground that something doesn't go wrong."

Toppleton was a small country town about three miles from Birch Dene, inhabited mainly by hand-loom weavers, factory hands, and innkeepers. Mr. Ruberry drove to 'The Roundabout'—a quaint old inn, with mullioned windows framed in ivy, high-pitched gables, and a ponderous nail-studded door.

After giving his horse in charge of the ostler, and ordering him a feed, Mr. Ruberry went into the bar and ordered a "drop" of whisky for his own consumption—partly, as he put it to himself, to keep the cold out, partly to keep his courage up ; for the idea of conducting his own case somewhat perturbed his mind, and he began to wish that he had retained 'Torney Bruff—his brother to the contrary notwithstanding. But it was too late now, and when the whisky had taken effect his spirits revived, and, telling Robin to "Come on," he led the way towards the court-house—a big room over the shop of the leading corn-chandler. There they found Blincoe and the two constables ; a gorgeously-arrayed beadle, who stood sentinel over a scared-looking young woman with a small baby, and a public, consisting of two old women and three dirty boys.

Presently the clerk came in, followed at a short interval by two magistrates, who took their seats, figuratively on the bench—literally on two of several ancient arm-chairs, with dilapidated cushions. One of them (the magistrates, not the chairs) was Major Dene. The name of the other was Dogwood, a corpulent gentleman, with an apoplectic face and out-starting eyes. But he was more generally called " A Nasty Conclusion," from a habit he had (when dispensing justice) of saying, " Don't let us come to an 'asty conclusion ;" and he was never known on such occasions to say aught else. Being the senior justice he took his seat on the centre chair, which was slightly higher than the others.

" Good morning, Mr. Ruberry," said Major Dene.

" Good morning, major," returned Ruberry.

Mr. Dogwood contented himself with a nod.

" What can we do for you, Mr. Ruberry ? "

asked the clerk. "Another runaway case, I suppose?"

"That and something more, Mr. Lush. The prisoner here has committed a runnery——"

"A runnery!"

"I mean a robbery. He's an apprentice of ours, and he not only ran away himself, but took a lot of things belonging to another apprentice, name of Nelson. He's here now"—(pointing to Robin)—"and he'll tell you all about it. I'm not much used to public speaking, and I don't know as it is necessary. It's a case for the assizes, I reckon."

"What is the nature of the articles alleged to have been stolen, and their value?"

"Clothes, wearing apparel, and books—ay, and there's a valise. As for their value, I should say at the very least they were worth ten pounds."

"Where were they taken from?"

"From the apprentice house."

"So! It is a case of felony, then. But all this is not evidence. We must have the prosecutor—what is his name? Nelson?—

thank you. We must have him sworn. Step
forward, Nelson, and take the book in your
right hand."

Robin stepped forward, looking pale and
rather agitated, yet as if he had made up his
mind to some very decided course.

"Take the book!" repeated the clerk.
"You—what is your name?"

"You said just now I was the prosecutor,"
observed Robin, with seeming irrelevance.

"So you are. Mr. Ruberry stated the case
on your behalf—at any rate, I presume so.
Take the book——"

"It is a mistake. I am not the prosecutor,
and I will not be the prosecutor. I have got
my things back. I have nothing against the
prisoner. I decline to give evidence."

All this was said in a breath.

"What the devil!" exclaimed Mr. Ruberry;
and then, feeling as if he was like to choke
with indignation and surprise, he stopped
short.

"Don't let us come to an 'asty conclusion,"
remarked Mr. Dogwood.

"If Nelson refuses to prosecute and give evidence, the case falls to the ground—doesn't it, Mr. Lush?" said Major Dene.

"I suppose so; but it is a very serious case, you know. Stealing from a dwelling-house is a capital felony. It is a case the Crown would, of course, take up."

"That's what my brother said," broke in Mr. Ruberry. "Cannot you make the young beggar prosecute, Mr. Lush?"

"I am afraid not. This court has no power to force a man to prosecute. Besides, if Nelson gave his evidence unwillingly, what would be the use? He might say that the prisoner took the things with his consent."

"The young villain! Why didn't you say you wouldn't prosecute before we started, Nelson, instead of bringing me here on a dead horse?"

"You never asked me, Mr. Ruberry; and I was not sure, until I heard this gentleman say I was the prosecutor, that I had any voice in the matter."

"What is your reason for not wanting

to prosecute, Nelson?" asked Major Dene, kindly; and Robin inferred from the magistrate's manner that he had his sympathy and approval.

"Because I would rather lose my right hand than be the means of getting Blincoe hanged, or anybody else. He is very unfortunate, and is sorry for taking my things. He has asked my forgiveness, and I have forgiven him. How can I ask for him to be punished after I have forgiven him?"

"I think you are quite right, Nelson. Were I in your place, I should do exactly the same. Is there any use pressing Nelson to prosecute, Mr. Ruberry? You surely don't want this poor devil to be hanged? He is only a lad, and I am sure after the lesson he has had, will not repeat the offence."

"Well, if you think so, major"—(hesitatingly)—"I don't care much about it either way. My brother thought if Blincoe were hanged it would be a good example for the other apprentices—that is all."

"A very bad example, I should say.

Wouldn't it be quite a sufficient example to give him a short term of imprisonment for running away?"

"Maybe it would; and it seems to me—as Nelson won't prosecute—it's about all as we can do. Ay, give him a month or two for that."

"What is your opinion, Mr. Dogwood?" inquired Major Dene, turning to his colleague, whose eyes were closed, as it might seem, in deep thought.

"Don't let us come to an 'asty conclusion," muttered the senior magistrate, waking up from his nap with a start.

"You agree with me then?"

Mr. Dogwood nodded his head, and reclosed his eyes.

The charge having been made in due form, and Blincoe admitting that he had run away, he was sentenced to a month's imprisonment.

"Are you going to the 'Roundabout,' Mr. Ruberry?" asked Major Dene, when the business was concluded.

"Yes, I always put up at the 'Roundabout.'"

"Well, I shall be there myself shortly, and if you are not gone, I should like to have a word or two with you."

"Certainly, Major Dene. I'm in no hurry. I'll wait till you come," returned the other, with deference; for the major was the great man of the neighbourhood, and Ruberry had special reason for desiring to "keep in" with him.

Before leaving the court-room, Robin shook hands with Blincoe.

"I suppose you are not very sorry?" he said.

"Sorry! No, I'm fain. It'll be the first holiday I've had since I was an apprentice. I wish they had made it two months instead of one."

On the way to the inn Ruberry said very little to Robin. Everything considered, he was by no means dissatisfied with the result of his amateur advocacy, albeit he had made up his mind never to repeat the experiment. The idea of prosecuting Blincoe for felony was Robert's, not his, and when he thought

of the ill-will they would not improbably
have incurred had Blincoe been prosecuted
to conviction, he was by no means sorry
the lad had escaped. More than one newspaper had lately called attention to the
treatment of factory apprentices by their
masters; the subject had even been mentioned
in Parliament; and "Old Ben" had a whole-
some regard for public opinion, being in this
respect both wiser and more susceptible than
his brother. Then, again, he had obliged
Major Dene, and he wanted to oblige Major
Dene. So, for the present at least, Robin
did not get the scolding which he expected,
and which he had nerved himself to take
without flinching, and, as he hoped, without
resenting.

While he waited in the bar-parlour Mr.
Ruberry regaled himself, and treated Robin,
with bread and cheese and ale—less, however,
out of any feeling of hospitality than that
he might keep the apprentice under his eye.
Even as it was, he would have a bad quarter
of an hour with his brother, and if by any

chance he returned without Nelson, he would never hear the last of it.

Mr. Ruberry had longer to wait than he expected, and when Major Dene appeared he had lighted a pipe, and was half way through a second pint of the 'Roundabout's' home-brewed.

"I am sorry I have kept you waiting," said the major. "Lush had some papers for me to sign, and detained me longer than I counted on. Thank you. I will have a glass of ale. . . . I wanted to speak to you——"

Here he paused and glanced at Robin, who, inferring therefrom that his absence was more desired than his company, made towards the door.

"Don't go far away," continued Major Dene. "I want a word with you also. You behaved very well to-day. I should have been sorry if we had had to send that poor devil to the assizes."

"It is about Nelson I want to speak to you," he resumed, when Robin was out of earshot. " A very unusual sort of apprentice, isn't he ? "

" Very. Seems clever and that, and writes an uncommonly good hand. He knows a lot about books too. You heard how boldly he spoke up just now. Gad! I was never so much surprised in my life."

" Yes, he spoke as boldly as he acted the other day. Now, when a lad both speaks boldly and acts fearlessly, you may depend on it there's something in him. Seeing, moreover, that in both cases he was exerting himself for others, he must be of a generous, unselfish disposition. And he looks it. Don't you think it would be worth your while to put him in some better position than that of a common apprentice ? It seems a waste of good material to make a mere factory hand of him."

" So it does. Still, you know, I don't quite see what else we can do with him. However, I'll think about it, and speak to my brother. It is more in his way than mine. He takes most of the management. I look after the books and outside matters. I think I shall retire before long, major. I'm getting tired of cotton spinning. It's a bothering business, and as I've no son to succeed me, and I've quite enough for my daughter and myself, I don't see why I should go on working to the end of my days."

"Well, I don't think I should if I were you. I hear your daughter is coming home. She will be a pleasant companion for you."

"Ay, she's coming home in a month or two"—(smiling)—"and right glad I shall be. I have only seen her six times in seven years. But she has got a good education—that is one comfort. I fear, though, she will find it dull work, poor lass, living with two old fellows like my brother and me, after being so long in London."

"Oh, I don't know. It is quite possible she may prefer a country life to town life. You must bring her to the Hall one of these days."

"Thank you kindly, major. I'm sure she will be very glad," said Mr. Ruberry, with a look of intense gratification. "She will have very little company, and hasn't a single female relative—except her Aunt Branscombe, and she won't see much of her."

"I suppose you will bring her out with the harriers sometimes?"

"Well, I think I shall. She can ride, and that old horse of mine—Tommy—will carry her first-rate. He's as clever as a cat and as safe as houses; you've only to let him have his head, and he'll carry you over owt. And as for this Nelson, as you seem to take so much interest in him, I've just been thinking that I might, maybe, find him a place in the counting-house. But as he's a scholar, and has a head for figures, it might be better for him in the end to let him learn the business thoroughly, and train him up as a manager. He'd be a made man then. I'll speak to my brother about it, and see what we can do. That was a shrewd remark you made just now, major, about waste of material. There's not much sense in putting a blood-horse between a pair of cart-shafts."

"Nor any gain, Mr. Ruberry. The lad is well-bred, unless I am much mistaken, and if you treat him fairly he will serve you well."

Meanwhile Robin was loitering about the inn door, contemplating the High-street of Toppleton, and mentally comparing it with Holborn, rather, as may be imagined, to the disadvantage of Toppleton. While he was thus occupied, a carriage with four horses and two postillions turned the corner and stopped before the 'Roundabout.' In the carriage were a lady and a little boy.

The lady put her head out of the window, and asked Robin if he knew where Major Dene was.

Robin doffed his hat, made a polite bow, and answered that Major Dene was at that moment in the bar-parlour with Mr. Ruberry.

"Will you kindly tell him that I am going to the other end of the town, and will call for him as I come back—in about ten minutes?"

"With pleasure, madam. But who shall

I say sends the message? I have not the pleasure——"

"Don't you know? I am Mrs. Dene, of Birch Dene Hall;" and there was a slight lifting of the eyebrows, and a gesture expressive of mild surprise that anybody at Toppleton should have to ask who she was.

And then she drew in her head, the four horses sprang forward, the carriage rattled up the street, and Robin returned to the bar-parlour to deliver his message.

"My wife!" said Major Dene. "Yes, I was expecting her. I walked in this morning, and it was agreed that she should call for me. I have been talking to Mr. Ruberry about you, Nelson, and he may possibly do something for you——"

"Well, we shall see," struck in Ruberry. "I make no promise, but if he's a good lad, we may happen put him forward. I will speak to my brother about him."

"And I have no doubt he will be a good lad, and deserve all you may do for him. Here"—taking Robin's arm and leading him towards the outer door—"you refused the money I offered you the other day because you hesitated to take a reward for doing a generous act. Take this as a simple gift—to oblige me. Put it in your pocket, and say no more about it. You will find it useful; money always is useful."

This time Robin did not refuse. Murmuring a "Thank you kindly, sir," he put the guinea in his pocket.

They were now outside, and the carriage was in sight. When it stopped, Mrs. Dene nodded, smiling, to her husband, and held her son up to the window to look at his father.

"Are you ready?" she asked. "How do you do?"—moving to Ruberry, who stood, hat in his hand, and otherwise in a rather cringing attitude. "Ah, there is the youth who asked me my name."

"Asked you your name, Edith!"

"Oh, I don't mean that he did it rudely—quite the reverse! I told him to let you know that I had called, and would call again.

It is the first time I was ever asked my name, though."

"Well, you can hardly expect everybody to know it by intuition; and as Nelson has been only a few days in the neighbourhood, his ignorance was quite excusable, I think. You must come up to the Hall some day, Nelson, and look round the gardens and the stables."

Although the invitation, if invitation it could be called, did not seem to amount to much, Robin, of course, gave the answer which courtesy required, and the major, after shaking hands with Mr. Ruberry, joined his wife and son, and the carriage drove off.

CHAPTER VI.

A FRATERNAL QUARREL.

"THAT is the lad I was telling you about, who so bravely stopped a runaway horse," said Major Dene, as he took his little boy between his knees.

"But you said he was an apprentice."

"So he is—in Ruberry's factory."

"Why, he has quite the air of a gentleman's son—wears well-fitting clothes, and does not seem in the least *gauche!*"

"True; and better still, he has generous instincts and a noble disposition. You should have seen how bravely he stood up in court to-day, and refused point-blank to prosecute a poor devil of an apprentice whom the Ruberrys wanted to hang. I cannot understand how he came to be an apprentice. He told me something of his story, and I am disposed to think that he has been sent down here to get him out of the way."

"To what end?"

"That is more than I can say. He spoke of a benefactor in London who had befriended him, and of somebody who sent him here, as I gathered, under false pretences, but he did not say a word about his family."

"Dear me! All this is quite mysterious, and I delight in mysteries. Perhaps he is a lost heir. When he comes to the Hall we must find out all about him."

"If he likes to tell us. I don't think it would be right to press him. And that reminds me of another matter. Mr. Ruberry's daughter is coming home shortly, and I want you to call there, and if she is a nice girl, have her up at the Hall occasionally."

"I call on the Ruberrys! You forget, Eustace, that they are tradespeople."

"So they are, in a sense; and, for that matter, so are we. They sell calicoes, and I sell coals and slate."

"But that is very different!"

"There is a difference, certainly. They make calicoes and I don't make coals and slate. They do their business in person; I do mine by deputy."

"So you think the Ruberrys are as good as we are! Why, Eustace, you are becoming more a Jacobin than ever!"

"Am I? It doesn't look like it"—and he laughingly pointed to the four thoroughbreds which were carrying them swiftly towards the noble Elizabethan mansion, whose high-pitched gables could be seen in the distance—"it doesn't look like it; while as for the Ruberrys being as good as we are—well, I don't like to make invidious distinctions. I am, however, free to confess that I don't admire them much. Their ideals are low, and Robert Ruberry has the name of being a tyrant with his work-people. On the other hand, they are neighbours, and come of a good old yeoman family, with whom the Denes have been on friendly terms for generations. And I don't ask you to associate with the two old men—I don't think I should care to associate with them myself; I only ask you to call on Miss Ruberry."

"Certainly, dear, as you wish it; and if I find her to be agreeable and well-educated, I will take her up. But why this sudden interest in Miss Ruberry? Did you ever see her?"

"No. She has been a long time in London—at school, I think; lost her mother when she was little more than a baby, and, as her father said just now, she is likely to have rather a dull life of it with these two old men. It would be a charity to call on her, and have her up to luncheon now and then—always provided, of course, that she is presentable and well-mannered, which you will soon see. And to be perfectly frank with you, I have another reason. The father would esteem any attention from you a great honour; it would please him immensely——"

"So he, at least, doesn't think that the Denes and the Ruberrys are on the same social level."

"I am sure he doesn't—fortunately for my present object——"

"Which is?"

"To do a good turn to Nelson."

"Do a good turn to Nelson! You talk in riddles, Eustace."

"It is an easy riddle to read, though. Ruberry knows that I take an interest in the lad, and if you do him the favour of calling on his daughter he may be induced to treat Nelson more kindly than he otherwise would."

"How deep you are, dear! Really, you know, this is becoming quite exciting—a mystery, a lost heir, and now a plot. All about a factory boy too! But you always had a weakness for boys, I think."

"Especially for fatherless and motherless boys who are cast adrift on the world, like this Nelson," said the major, gravely. "Imagine our little Willy in a similar position!"

"Oh, Eustace, don't suggest anything so dreadful!" exclaimed Mrs. Dene, snatching up her boy and covering him with kisses. "No such fate could befall my darling Willy

—the heir to Birch Dene. You are right, dear. It is our duty to do what we can for the lad. We will have him at the Hall. I am sure he looks a great deal more gentlemanlike than Mr. Ruberry."

As the Denes were driving home in their carriage, Mr. Ruberry, accompanied by Robin, was driving home in his gig.

The senior partner being slightly " sprung " with his two pints of beer and two glasses of whisky (he had taken a second as a stirrup cup), and, elated by the major's invitation, was in great spirits, talked incessantly and rather boastfully, also with much less caution than he had observed during the interview in the bar-parlour. He assured Robin that he loved him as his own son, and would make a man of him; talked about his daughter, protesting that she was the finest lass in those parts. He had brought her up as a lady, and when the time came he meant her to marry a gentle-man—" a real gentleman, of good family and ancient lineage; none of your mushrooms sprung from a dunghill." He could give

Miriam thirty thousand pounds, and have as much left for himself—which was more than many a man with a handle to his name could do for his child. And as there was nobody else for his brother's money, and Robert was even better off than himself, the lass had a right to look high, and was as good as Mrs. Dene any day, though she was an Arnside of Morecambe, while as for the major——

At this point Mr. Ruberry's outpouring suddenly ceased and his countenance fell, for, catching sight of his factory chimney in the near distance, he bethought him that he was talking rather at random, and that he had still to give an account of himself and the events of the day to his strong-minded and somewhat despotic brother.

"This is all between ourselves, Nelson," he said, earnestly. "Not a word of what I have been saying to anybody—to anybody, mind that. Keep a still tongue, and I'll be your friend, as I promised Major Dene. But you may have to wait a while. My brother may not be of my mind just at first—and he manages the factory, you know. Mum's the word, mind, or it may go ill with you."

When they reached the mill gates Mr. Ruberry told Robin to take the gig "round to the stable," and then, descending from the vehicle, bent his steps towards the counting house.

"Now for a rumpus!" he muttered between his set teeth. "Well, the sooner we get it over the better, I reckon."

Robert, who looked as fluffy as if he had just emerged from a bale of his own "raw material," was examining and valueing cotton samples. As his brother entered the office he turned sharply round, and pushed his spectacles up on his forehead.

"So you've got back!" he said. "How went you on?"

"Middling. They've given him a month for running away," replied Benjamin, coming to the point at once.

"And what have they given him for the burglary?"

"Nowt."

"Nowt! What mean you? How was that?"

"Nelson refused to give evidence."

"Just like his impudence! What the devil for, I should like to know?"

"He said he wouldn't be the means of getting Blincoe hanged."

"But I want Blincoe to be hanged. Curse Nelson! Why didn't you make him give evidence?"

"How could I make him? And Major Dene thought it was better not to press the matter; and after such an expression of opinion from the bench, I thought so too."

"You thought so too, did you? So Nelson wasn't so much to blame, after all. It was you and your friend, Major Dene, that put him up not to give evidence, and a nice mess you have made of it, one way and another. We shall be laughing-stocks for all the countryside. Beaten by a bit of a Cockney apprentice! If you had engaged Bruff, as I wanted you, this would never have happened."

Though Benjamin generally let his brother have his way, because being himself of an easy-going nature, he found submission easier than resistance, and disliked contention, and for other good and sufficient reasons, there were limits to his endurance, and the limit had now been overpassed. To be reproached for not doing the very thing which he had reluctantly refrained from doing, at Robert's own instance, was more than flesh and blood could bear.

"What the deuce do you mean?" he cried, angrily. "It was just the other way about. I wanted to engage Bruff, and you would not let me. And it isn't the first time, either, that you have blamed me for following your advice when things have not turned out as you wanted. It is time an end was put to this, Robert. You forget, I think, that I am your elder brother and the head of the firm. I am glad Blincoe has got off, and I am pleased that Nelson behaved as he did. I should have put my foot down at first, and refused either to take Blincoe to Toppleton or let him be prosecuted. The next time you want to hang an apprentice you'll have to do it yourself. It is true what people say about you, Robert. You are a hard taskmaster, and if you don't alter, it will be the worse for us both."

" You are in a passion, I think," said Robert, taken aback by this unexpected outburst.

" Well, haven't I a right to be ? You'd provoke a saint, and I never pretended to be more than a good churchman. You are too hard and domineering, and you get worse ; and no good will come of it, mark me if there does. I dare say you will be vexed, but you began, and I mean to have my say out while I am at it. Now, there's that Nelson. I am not going to have him punished or ill done to, or owt o' that sort, on account of what's happened to-day."

" Who's going to do ill to him ? A lad as can lick Black Jack in an up-and-down fight may be trusted to take care of himself, I think."

" Did he lick Jack ? I had not heard. Ay, he's a lad of spirit. Major Dene said so today. The major takes a great interest in him. Couldn't we turn Nelson to better account than making a common piecer of him, Robert

He's a good scholar, and nobody can deny as
he's clever."

" Ay, too clever by half. Do with the lad
what you like. Feed him on turtle and cham-
pagne, clothe him in purple and fine linen,
make a gentleman of him, and wed him to
your Miriam, if you like. I don't care a brass
farthing. But I know one thing—no good
will come of it. However, it's nowt to me.
You're my elder brother, and head of the firm,
and can do as you like, I suppose. What is
the use of asking me? Only mind one thing.
The concern mustn't suffer—not for all the
majors and apprentices in creation!"

And with that "Owd Bob" dashed his
spectacles on the desk, put his hands in his
pockets, and rushed out of the office in a huff.

It were hard to say which of the two
brothers was the more surprised by the result of this encounter, for never before had
Ben so resolutely resisted his junior's dictation,
or come off so completely victorious. As a
rule, he came off the reverse of victorious,
partly, as has been already hinted, owing to

the easiness of his temper, partly because he knew by experience that Robert's judgment on matters of business was generally sounder than his own, and that to Robert's energy and hard-headedness their common prosperity was mainly due.

The relations between the brothers were somewhat remarkable. Their father had been a yeoman and a farmer at a time when agriculture was the most flourishing of English industries, and they inherited from him several hundred acres of good land and a fair amount of ready money. Benjamin would have followed in the old man's footsteps, and stuck to the land. Robert, on the other hand, was eager to embark in the new business of cotton spinning. The elder reluctantly consented, and Birch Dene Mill was built and filled with the best machinery of the period. Into this enterprise the younger brother threw himself with almost preternatural energy. He spared neither himself nor others—"following the work," as the saying is, from morning to night, literally dividing his time between factory and bed. When not asleep—and he never slept long—he was at work. His sole indulgence was an extra glass of grog on Saturday night, and staying in bed until breakfast-time on Sunday morning. This devotion to business, practised at first as a duty, ended in becoming so entirely a second nature that, outside his factory gates, Robert Ruberry was never content. He had been heard to say that, except to "clean up," and let the bearings cool, machinery should never be allowed to stop. Twice in twenty-five years he had ventured to take a holiday for the benefit of his health, but unable to bear separation from his beloved factory, and fearing that in his absence the business would go to the devil, he returned on each occasion in less than a week, declaring that nothing should ever induce him to repeat the experiment.

Yet " Owd Bob " was by no means a miser. He made money because he could not help it —he had no other pleasure—and saved because, as he said, he had no time to spend.

But when his brother married, Robert settled
five thousand pounds on the bride; he sub-
scribed a thousand towards the cost of the
war with France, and two or three sums of
five hundred each towards the building and
endowment of churches. As for his work-
people, however, it never occurred to him
that they had any other needs than plenty
of work and just enough wage to keep body
and soul together. He had a theory that the
less they earned the harder they wrought;
and on one occasion, being asked to put the
cottages in which they lived in a better state
of repair, answered that the cottages were
quite good enough to sleep in; their living
place was the factory.

The elder brother was a man of another
stamp. Though shrewd and keen, he pre-
ferred farming to spinning, liked better to
punch the ribs of a fat bullock than value
a sample of cotton, and spent money with
almost as much pleasure as he earned it.
Ben was looked upon, and looked upon himself, as the gentleman of the concern, attended

markets, pretended to keep the books, and managed the farm. He was fond of horses, hunted with the harriers, and liked to ride about, wearing a jockey cap and followed by a couple of dogs, like his father before him. When he married he enlarged and, as he thought, otherwise improved the old house, and Robert took up his abode in a double cottage near the factory gates; but after Mrs. Ruberry's death the brothers again lived together in the ancestral home.

The only child of the marriage was a girl, and when she was ten years old, her father, after several unsatisfactory experiments with nursery governesses and lady housekeepers, took the sensible course of sending Miriam to her Aunt Branscombe, in London, who had offered to superintend her education. There she remained nearly seven years, and Mrs. Branscombe would fain have had her stay longer. But Mr. Ruberry yearned for his daughter's company. He thought that with his help she would be quite competent to undertake the management of his house, and, as he had informed Major Dene, she was expected at Birch Dene in the course of a month or two.

This was the state of things when the two brothers had their first serious difference, and the elder was left free to deal with Robin as he thought fit.

CHAPTER VII.

ROBIN AT CHURCH.

RICH once more, Robin should have been happy, but before Major Dene's guinea had been in his possession many minutes, it began to breed him trouble. He was so afraid of losing it that, during the ride home, he kept the coin in his hand and his hand in his pocket. But this could not go on for ever, and while he drove the gig to the stables (at Mr. Ruberry's house) he was obliged to let the guinea take care of itself, which fortunately it did. How to dispose of it when he went to work was the next question. To take it with him would be to ensure its loss, the pockets of his working breeches being full of holes; while to leave it behind, whether in his valise or elsewhere, would be running a big risk. It might go the way of his other money, and Robin, schooled by experience, was growing preternaturally cautious. After long thought he came to the conclusion that the only safe course was to place the guinea in the hands of somebody who had a strong-box, and could be trusted to return it upon demand.

Mr. Ruberry! Yes, why should he not make Mr. Ruberry his banker. He seemed very friendly at present, and there was a big iron safe in the counting-house, where he felt sure his fortune would be quite safe. But suppose, when he required it for the expenses of the journey to Portsmouth, which he still contemplated, Mr. Ruberry should make difficulties, or ask awkward questions? How then? No, this plan would not do at all.

Old Dick! He seemed honest, was kind in his own rugged fashion, and evidently held Robin in high respect for his clerkly qualities. Unfortunately, however, Dick, like everybody else at Birch Dene, was fond of drink, and Robin had a strong suspicion that if he entrusted him with his guinea it would all go down his throat. No, Dick would not do either.

But—happy thought!—old Betty might. She was at least as honest as her husband; she did not drink, and if she had not a strong-box, she had probably an old stocking, or some other secret receptacle, where the guinea could be safely put away.

So on his return to the apprentice house to change his Sunday suit for his working garments, Robin broached the subject to the old woman—nobody being present but themselves.

" You've getten a guinea!" she exclaimed, with . a gesture of surprise. " Major Dene's gav' you a guinea! Why, it is one pound one! It's more than a spinner addles in a week, and happen three or four childer to keep. Nobody ever gav' me a shilling, let alone a guinea. But they do say as Major Dene is very fluent wi' his brass. Keep it for you! But where mon I keep it? . . . I'll tell you what I'll do, if you like: I'll

stitch it i' my stays. It's about th' last
place where onybody would look for a gowd
piece, and as I wears 'em all day, and they
lie on a chair by my bedside all neet, I don't
think they are like to get stown. But if
they do, I'se not be answerable. You'll mind
that, Nelson—I'se not be answerable."

To this condition Robin gladly assented.
It was to the last degree improbable that
anybody would steal the old woman's stays,
and he went to his work with a lighter heart
than he had known since he became a factory
lad. His prospects were brightening : he had
saved Blincoe from being hanged, and recovered his clothes, and, thanks to Major
Dene's gift, he possessed the nucleus of a
fund which would enable him, if he. kept in
the same mind, and a favourable opportunity
should present itself, to leave Birch Dene and
go in search of his father—so soon as he could
think of his name. He did not put much trust
in Mr. Ruberry's promises, and was firmly
resolved to remain an inmate of the apprentice
house no longer than he could possibly help.

On the Saturday night he received his wage—one shilling. Jim Rabbits, who paid him, mentioned that it was not customary to pay apprentices until they had been at work three months, and even then they generally began with sixpence. But "Owd Ben" had ordered that he should have a shilling "from the start."

"I never knowed it done afore," said the spinning master. "That comes of your being so larned. Not as a shilling a week is much for a schollard like you. All th' same, it's better than a punch on th' shins wi' an iron clog, and it shows as Ben thinks well on you. That's summat." And then he tendered Robin twopence as an honorarium for his lessons, and invited him to breakfast at his house on the following morning.

Robin took the coppers and accepted the invitation. He wanted money, and was getting tired of porridge.

Rabbits had a managing little wife, two children, and a roomy cottage with a small parlour. The breakfast, greatly enjoyed by

Robin, was a substantial meal of black-puddings and fried eggs, washed down with small beer. Coffee was too costly for common use, and the Birch Dene people only indulged in tea (diluted with rum) on festive occasions, or when they felt out of sorts—which, for some reason or another, generally happened on Mondays.

The morning was given to a reading and writing lesson, to which the spinning master applied himself so energetically that he had to take off his coat and roll up his shirt-sleeves, and he declared that learning to be a scholar was the hardest work he had ever tried.

After dinner they took a walk in the fields, which Robin enjoyed even more than he had enjoyed the black-puddings and fried eggs. The other apprentices spent the morning, some of them the entire day, in bed—which, seeing how hard they were compelled to work during the week, was perhaps the best thing they could do. Those who felt so disposed were allowed to play at "blackthorn," tag-rag, marbles, or anything they liked, in the factory yard, but were never allowed to go outside unaccompanied by Dick or the watchman.

A few Sundays later Robin breakfasted as before with Jim Rabbits, and they were in the midst of a lesson when the spinning master—who was trying his hand at writing large M's—threw down his pen and proposed that they should go to church.

"Ay, let's go," he repeated earnestly. "I can howd th' prayer-book reyt end up now, and I said as I'd ne'er put my yed in a church ageean till I could."

Robin looking rather mystified, Rabbits explained that the last of the few times he had ever been to church (some two years previously), "an owd mon wi' a big stick" politely gave him what Rabbits presumed to be a prayer-book, which (not liking to make a public exhibition of his ignorance) he took, and made as if he could read, and was following the parson. As ill-luck would have it, however, somebody who could read noticed that he held the book wrong side up, and afterwards unfeelingly bruited the fact abroad as an excellent joke, thereby causing the poor fellow to be unmercifully chaffed, or, as he put it, "trotted."

"Damum!" he said, bitterly; "they geet agate a-calling me 'Top-end-up' one while!"

So they went to Birch Dene church—a hideous concern with slab sides and a squat steeple, towards the building of which the brothers Ruberry had contributed five hundred pounds a piece. The pews for the commonalty were high-backed, with narrow, uncushioned seats; the pulpit was a huge three-decked affair, the lowest tier being occupied by a clerk with a red nose and a cracked voice. When the service began Robin found the place for his companion, but, prompted by a spirit of mischief, put the prayer-book into his hand wrong side up. After a puzzled stare, Jim, with an *Et tu, Brute* look, turned the book round, and tried diligently to follow the parson—though he made rather a stern chase of it, being always a long way behind.

Then, for the first time, Robin looked round. On either side of the three-decked pulpit was a large State pew, lined with green baize, comfortably cushioned, and strewn with hassocks. One was occupied by Major Dene, his wife, and another lady. Mrs. Dene was a tall, fine-looking woman, with a healthy colour, soft brown eyes, and a comely countenance, albeit the expression of it was somewhat haughty and reserved. A profusion of chestnut ringlets shaded her face, her hat (hats were in fashion) was adorned with drooping ostrich feathers, and she wore a black satin gown, richly trimmed with lace.

In the other State pew were the brothers Ruberry and a young girl. Old Bob was so transformed that Robin hardly knew him. His calves were clothed in black silk stockings, his shoe-buckles were of silver, his yellow waistcoat and ample blue coat were resplendent with gilded buttons, and on his nose was perched a pair of gold-rimmed spectacles. He looked intensely respectable and devout, followed the sermon with close attention, and

made the responses in a loud voice and with
seeming fervour.

" By gum, there's Owd Bob ! What's made
him buck hissel' up i' that fashion, I wonder ? "
whispered Rabbits. " I haven't seen him i'
that coat sin his brother wor wed."

But just then Robin had eyes only for the
young girl. Her face was the most winsome
he had ever seen—oval, with violet eyes, a
fair skin, straight nose, dainty lips, and a
dimpled chin. It wore an expression of sweet
gravity befitting the place and the occasion.
Though she was somewhat below middle
height, her figure was shapely, and her move-
ments were graceful and unconstrained. This
young girl's attire was of an almost Puritan
simplicity. The sole ornament of her velvet
hat was a scarlet ribbon ; her gown was silver
gray ; her beautiful arms were bare to the
shoulder ; her hair, glossy black, was con-
fined by a velvet band ; and a coral neck-
lace, with a golden clasp, encircled her shapely
throat.

" That's th' lass," whispered the spinning

master. " It's for her as Owd Bob has bucked
hissel' up so."

" That must be Miriam," thought Robin ;
and happening to look at the same time
towards the Dene Hall pew, he noticed that
Major Dene was gazing intently, and with
troubled eyes, at Mr. Ruberry's daughter.

Then the sermon began, and save the three-
decked pulpit, the tops of a few tall men's
heads, and the backs of a few tall women's
bonnets, nothing was to be seen. After trying
to puzzle out the text (found for him by
Robin), Jim Rabbits composed himself to
sleep. Robin, though he felt drowsy, made
a strong effort to keep awake ; but the sermon,
delivered in an almost inaudible monotone,
was too much for him—it had the same soporific
effect as a nurse's lullaby or the babbling of
a distant brook—and he, too, made an excur-
sion into the land of dreams. When he
awoke, the rector, undisturbed by a few snores,
was calmly saying, " And now, sixthly, my
brethren "—from which the young fellow
rightly inferred that he had been asleep rather

a long time. A few minutes later the sermon came to an end, and Rabbits, roused by a furtive pinch from Robin, wakened up with a start.

" Bithmon ! " he exclaimed ; " I do believe I've been asleep ! "

The rector frowned visibly, old people stared, young ones tittered, and the spinning master, to his utter confusion, became the cynosure of every eye.

" I shall never hear the last of this," he murmured ; and as the old clerk uttered the final " Amen," Jim hurried out of church, painfully conscious of the fact that he had committed an offence for which ability to hold his prayer-book right side up would not be considered a sufficient atonement.

Robin followed at his leisure, not leaving his pew until the great folks had left theirs. When he reached the porch Mrs. Dene was getting into her carriage, while the Major was talking to Mr. Ruberry ; but Robin observed that he looked more at the daughter than the father, and with the same wistful expression as before. As he was about to join his wife, he caught Robin's eye, and returned his greeting with a friendly nod.

"I like Miss Ruberry," said Mrs. Dene, making room for her husband, "and I shall take her up. She has rather a sweet face, don't you think?"

"I call it a very sweet face. Why didn't you stay and let her be introduced to you?"

"I hate being introduced to people at church. All the rustics stop to stare and listen; but I shall call."

"When?"

"When we come back from York; I shall not have time before. I say, Eustace."

"Yes, Edith."

"Did you ever notice your *protégé's* head?"

"My *protégé's* head! What on earth do you mean?"

"That factory boy you take so much interest in—Mr. Ruberry's apprentice. The lost heir, you know."

"Oh, Nelson! No, I don't think I ever

noticed his head much. Is there anything wrong with it ?"

"Not wrong. It is strange, though. While in church he generally stood with his back to our pew—I think he was looking at Miss Ruberry—and I noticed above his right ear something white, which at first I took for a piece of cotton ; but I soon saw that it was a lock of white hair. That is very unusual, is it not ?—a white lock on a nearly black head, and so young a head too !"

"Unusual, certainly, yet not so much so as you might think. There was a fellow in my regiment who had a black head which was simply fringed with white locks. Over the right ear, did you say ?"

"Yes, over the right ear."

"I will make a point of looking at it the next time I see Nelson. It is strange that so marked a peculiarity escaped me. But though I am rather given to the study of faces, I am not in the habit of paying much attention to heads."

This seemed to exhaust the subject; Mrs.

Dene made no further remark, and her husband, turning to the window, pensively contemplated the landscape.

When they alighted from the carriage she went straightway to the nursery, like the good mother she was; he to his own room. Like the house of which it formed a part, this room was quaint, old, and picturesque. The walls were wainscotted, the windows deeply embayed. Over the carved oak mantelpiece was the stuffed head of a wolf which the major had killed in Spain, surmounted by a trophy of arms, and the dinted cuirass of a French dragoon, whom he had slain in single combat at Waterloo. At one end of the room was a well-furnished gun-rack; at the other a well-filled bookcase, flanked by an ancient brass-bound desk; in the middle, a large table, on which were works of reference, packets of official-looking documents, writing materials, and a pair of double-branched silver candle-sticks.

Major Dene, after locking the door, un-locked the old desk, and from one of the

drawers he took a packet carefully wrapped
in tissue-paper. Then, seating himself at the
table, he proceeded to unfold the packet. It
contained a miniature, a lock of hair, and
several letters. Taking up the miniature, he
looked at it intently for several minutes.

"The likeness is wonderful," he murmured.
" It might be her own portrait, and yet there
can be no kinship. . . . It is quite impossible.
Poor girl! I wonder . . ."

Then he opened one of the letters, and, as
he read, heavy tears rolled down his cheeks
and fell on the paper.

A knock at the door.

" Yes. What is it ? "

" Luncheon is ready, Major Dene."

Hurriedly, and with trembling fingers, re-
folding the packet, he replaced it in the desk
and left the room.

CHAPTER VIII.

MIRIAM.

THE spinning master's cabin. Robin doing what appears to be a somewhat elaborate calculation. Rabbits, who holds in his hand a number of small wheels strung on a wire, watching him admiringly.

"A twenty-nine toothed pinion will do it," says the young man, looking up from his paper.

"I think I've getten it here," answers Jim, selecting one of the wheels and beginning to count the teeth. "Why, you're welly as sharp at sums as th' bookkeeper, and a good deal sharper than Owd Bob. Ben wor talking about you yesterday. He did not know till I towd him how good you are at ciphering. He says I mun put you up to all as I can,

and as you needn't spend all your time
piecing. You may go about a bit and help
me. I towd you how it would be, and after
a while you'll have to go in th' card-room,
and pyke up what you can there, and I mak'
no doubt as your wage 'll be raised afore long.
But it's ali Ben's doing. I wish it wor Bob's,
for your sake. It is him as is th' real mayster.
But he never mentions your name, and I
don't think he hoaf likes you. But that's
nowt. I don't think he likes owt but th'
factory and hissel', though some folks says as
he sets a deal o' store by Ben's lass. . . .
Hello! Who is there? What's up, I wonder?"

A sound of hurried footsteps, excited voices,
and a cry of pain, followed by the opening of
the door, and the appearance of two big lads,
who support between them a small boy.

"Little Harney's getten catched," they say,
pointing to the poor child's right hand, all
covered with blood.

"Little foo'! What has he been doing?
Bring him here, and let's see what it is,"
says Rabbits.

Robin takes the half-fainting child on his lap. He is one of the youngest and smallest of the apprentices who came with him from London.

"Won't you send for a doctor?"

"Nay, we mun have no doctor for a job like this. He's nobbut getten' two of his fingers smashed. I'll bind 'em up i' th' blood —Whitworth bottle and a rag—that'll about do this time, I reckon."

As Jim speaks, he reaches from the window-sill a bottle containing a red mixture, a few drops of which he lets fall on the wounded fingers. Harney moans pitifully.

"It keens a bit at fost, I know," continued the spinning master, "but it'll soon be o'er. There's nowt like Whitworth bottle for killing pain and making a cure."

And then, with strips of linen rag, he bandages the crushed fingers swiftly and deftly—for Jim, in his way, is quite an amateur surgeon.

Again Robin suggests that a doctor should be called in.

"I cannot, and Owd Bob willn't," says Rabbits. "If you wor to speak of such a thing to him, he'd go fair mad. It's the last shift when he sends for a doctor. Why, he'd charge hoaf a crown for one visit, and you may be sure he'd come seven or eight times, to say nowt o' bandages and bottles o' stuff. . . . Now"—(to Harney)—"thou can go and lake" [play]. "Thou'll do no more piecing for a week or two."

But the unfortunate child being still too faint to walk unaided, Robin raises him in his arms, and carries him to the apprentice house.

"Getten catched, has he?" exclaimed Betty. "They're allus getting catched. Two fingers! If it had been one, I should ha' said he'd happen done it o' purpose."

"On purpose! Why should the poor boy get himself hurt on purpose?"

"To get a holiday, to be sure. There was one lad geet catched so oft that Owd Bob ordered him to be weel hided every time, and have nowt to eat but skilly till he went back to his work. It cured him, that did; but he geet killed at last."

"How?"

"Put his yed between a pair o' big spur weels, and geet it ta'en off."

"Poor boy! But surely not on purpose, Jenny?"

"There wor them as thowt so—and it's like enough; he wor a queer lad. But th' crowner's quest wor accidental death; and it wouldn't do for any of us to say owt different, you know. Put Harney in this rocking-chair by th' fireside. He'll not want to run about much to-day, I reckon."

Neither that day nor the next was Harney able to run about much, or at all. He passed a wretched night, and in the morning seemed so weak and ill that Robin would not let him get up. On the following day he was no better, and though he rallied somewhat towards the end of the week, a change for the worse set in on the Saturday night, and Robin became seriously alarmed. On the Sunday morning he insisted that Dick should send for a doctor.

"I'se do nowt o' th' sort," said the old fellow, gruffly. "You may ax Owd Bob, if you like; but I can tell you aforehand what he'll say: 'Let him dee; he's nobbut a 'prentice, and I can get two fro' London for less than th' doctor will want, whether he cures him or not.'"

"I don't believe Mr. Robert is as bad as you say, Dick, and I am sure Mr. Ruberry isn't. At any rate, I shall go and ask them, and at once. I am sure Harney is very ill."

The Ruberrys were breakfasting at (for them) the unusually late hour of half-past eight. Miriam was at the head of the table, looking, in her neat print gown, as fresh and rosy as the morning itself. Her father was busy with his matutinal egg, and her uncle just finishing the dish with which he always began the day — porridge and ale — when the door opened, and a red-cheeked maid entered.

"There's a young mon fro' the factory wants to see you," she says—"name o' Nelson."

"Nelson! What does he want coming bothering of a Sunday morning?"

"I don't know; but he says it is very serious."

"Say we are all at breakfast, and let him wait in th' kitchen," answers Robert. "I'll come and see him directly."

"Nay, if it's serious, let us have him in and hear what it is," says Benjamin. "Tell him to come forrud, Phœbe."

So Robin was ushered in, and, after respectfully greeting his masters and the young lady, told his tale—how ill Harney had been, how much worse he was, and how serious were his symptoms, concluding with an urgent appeal that a doctor might be sent for while there was yet time.

"Nay, we willn't have a doctor just yet," said Robert. "We'll see how he is to-morrow."

"But suppose he dies to-day!"

"Well, there's plenty more where he comes from. He's only a bit of an apprentice."

"Oh, uncle, what are you saying?" ex-

claimed Miriam, with heightening colour and
indignant eyes. "Only an apprentice! Poor
child! Is he not one of God's creatures?
Has he not a soul? If he dies, the sin will
be at your door. You don't mean what you
say. You will send for a doctor. Do, please,
at once."

"We happen had better send for Radley,
Robert," suggested the elder brother.

"Ay, send for him, if you like," returned
Robert, with a somewhat disconcerted look.

The idea that an apprentice might have a
soul to be saved, as well as himself, had, so
to speak, taken the wind out of his sails.

"Shall I fetch him?" said Robin.

"Nay, we'll send Gib to Toppleton with
the gig, and then he can bring Radley back.
If we don't, he'll most likely not come
till towards night — and then worse for
drink."

With that Mr. Ruberry summoned Phœbe,
and sent the order to Gib. Robin bowed, and
made as if he would retire.

"Have you breakfasted?" asked Miriam.

Robin admitted that he had not breakfasted.

"Won't you have a cup of coffee? I'm
sure you must be hungry."

The brothers looked as if the world was
coming to an end; but as neither of them
liked to say Miriam nay, they made no
objection. Benjamin even seconded the
invitation.

"Ay, draw up to th' table, Nelson," he
said. "Take that egg; or you'd happen liefer
have a bit of this rasher."

"Give him both, father. He must be very
hungry after his walk. The air is sharp this
morning."

Robin, nothing loth, thanked his hostess,
and did as he was told. It seemed an age
since he had tasted coffee or enjoyed the
perfume of a rasher.

"It is very good of you to take so much
trouble about that poor boy," said Miriam.
"You belong to the factory, of course. What
are you?"

"Only an apprentice, Miss Ruberry."

"An apprentice! I thought the apprentices were all little."

"Not by any means. Some are nearly grown up. They remain apprentices until they are of age."

"And you are really one of them. Do you live in the apprentice house?"

"I am really one of them, and I live in the apprentice house."

"But you don't look—I mean I shouldn't have thought. . . Father, I want to go to the apprentice house and see what it is like, and this poor boy."

The brothers exchanged glances of dismay. Had Miriam proposed to become a common factory girl, and take up her abode at the apprentice house, they could not have looked more horrified.

"That would not do at all, Miriam; I could not allow it. It's quite out of the question, you know—quite out of the question," said Mr. Ruberry, when he had recovered from the confusion into which his daughter's extraordinary demand had thrown him. "Isn't it quite out of the question, Robert?"

"Quite. I never heard of such a thing in my life."

"But why is it out of the question?" asked Miriam, quietly, yet in a tone which showed that she had by no means abandoned her project.

"For many reasons. The lads are rough-spoken, and some of 'em never gets up of a Sunday. That is quite enough, if there were nowt else."

"But they will get up; I'll run down and make them get up," put in Robin, eagerly. "And Harney would be so pleased and proud —he is such a little fellow, and nobody to nurse him. He would think an angel had come to see him."

"That's all nonsense!" interposed Robert, impatiently. "It wouldn't do, I tell you. It would make 'em all think too much of themselves; they'd be past managing. And then. . . I don't think you should let her go, Benjamin—I really don't. Th' apprentice house is no fit place for a young gentle-woman."

Miriam rose from her chair, and going to her uncle, placed her hand on his shoulder.

"Uncle," she said, "suppose you were a little child once more, but without either father or mother, among strangers in a strange place, and sick perhaps unto death—would you like me to come and see you?"—(kissing him).

"That—that's hardly a fair question, I think, Miriam," stammered Old Bob, after vainly scrutinizing his inner consciousness for an answer to his niece's *argumentum ad hominem.*

"Yes, it is—quite fair; and I want you to answer it, as I am sure you will, honestly —would you like me to come and see you?"

"Ay, lass, I would; but . . ."

"That is enough. 'Whatsoever ye would that men should do to you, do ye even so unto them.' You were at church last Sunday, Uncle Robert, and you are going again to-day."

"We shall be like to let her have her way,
I think," said Ben, who was not altogether
displeased with his brother's discomfiture.

"It seems so; she's too many for us old
fellows," returned Robert, with a forced laugh.
"Run down to th' factory, Nelson. Make
th' lads wash and don theirselves, and tell
Dick and Betty as th' young missis is coming
to see Harney and look 'em up."

"Let him finish his breakfast first, uncle,"
said Miriam, with a pleasant smile. "He
has only just begun. Is your coffee quite
agreeable, Mr. Nelson?"

Robin blushed, and protested that it was
the most agreeable coffee he had ever tasted.

Old Bob made no further remark, but
looked unutterable things. The shock of hearing an apprentice addressed as "Mr.," and
asked whether his coffee was agreeable, had
reduced him for the moment to impotent
silence.

A few minutes later Robin, having drunk
a second cup of coffee, made his bow and
withdrew.

"You'll quite spoil that lad, Miriam. You'll spoil 'em all if you carry on in this way."

"How, Uncle Robert? What have I done wrong?"

"You called him 'Mr.,' and asked if his coffee was agreeable."

"And why not? He is well spoken, and behaves like a gentleman."

"I say nowt about that; but what I do say is as he's a hand, and hands are bad enough to manage as it is. If we don't rule 'em with a tight hand and keep 'em in their places, they'll be th' masters of us instead of us being th' masters of them."

"Couldn't you rule them by kindness, uncle?"

Robert, leaning back in his chair, laughed heartily.

"Rule 'em by kindness! Rule 'em by kindness! Who would be such a fool as to try, I should like to know? Where did you get your ideas, Miriam? Not from Aunt Branscombe, I reckon. I always thought she was a sensible woman."

"So she is, and a good woman. I owe her much. It was she who taught me that 'Love thy neighbour as thyself' means that we should love everybody—that every fellow-creature is a neighbour. You believe the Bible, Uncle Robert?"

This was taking him on his weak side, for he prided himself on being an orthodox Christian and a good Churchman, and though in his heart he strongly demurred to much of his niece's theology, fear of seeming to impugn the authority of the Old Book prevented him from contesting the point, and rendered his reply somewhat irrelevant.

"Of course I believe in the Bible. Whatever made you ask such a question?" he exclaimed, with more indignation than he felt. "Did you think I was an infidel? There's no infidels at Birch Dene, Miriam. If I heard a man say as he did not believe in the Bible, I should send him about his business that very minute, whoever he was."

"Do you think that would make him a believer, Uncle Robert?"

"That's more than I can say. But, whether or not, we'll have no infidels about us."

"Nor Jacobins neither," put in Ben. "They are just as bad. Ay, six of one and half a dozen of t'other. Jacobins generally are infidels, I think, and should be treated as traitors. However, there's neither on our ground, I am thankful to say; and I'll take care as there isn't."

After this the brothers drew up to the fire and lighted their pipes, and Miriam, who had household matters to attend to, and to prepare for the visit to the apprentice house, left them to themselves—an opportunity by which they profited to talk her over, as they had done nearly every day since her return. They could not make her out. It was not merely that she had gone away a frolicsome child and come back a comely young woman, with (as they deemed it) queer ways and a Cockney accent. This was to be expected. But she had also come back with ideas and a will of her own, together with a sweet imperiousness of manner which nobody seemed able to resist. Her father was as wax in her hands, and though Robert grumbled and protested, he mostly ended by submitting. In one respect she was a girl after his own heart—being active and energetic to a fault, and familiar with all the details of domestic economy. She had already assumed the management of the household—rather to the disgust of the servants, who, under Mr. Ruberry's rule, had done pretty much as they liked; for Ben was easy-tempered, and Robert never meddled with his brother's private concerns. Miriam declared that the house was positively dirty, and within a few days of her arrival there was such an overhauling and cleaning-up as there had not been for years. She was always doing something, and in the course of a few weeks revolutionized her father's establishment and renovated his house —not before they wanted it—and Old Bob was heard repeatedly to affirm that she had not an idle bone in her body.

Miriam's energy and brightness were native to her, but her love of order, her good sense, and most of the ideas which had so much startled her father and her uncle she owed to her Aunt Branscombe, under whose care she had passed the greater part of her conscious life. This lady, herself highly cultured, had married into a Quaker family, and albeit she did not formally join the Society of Friends, she approved of their principles and sympathized with their aims, was intimately acquainted with Clarkson, Wilberforce, and Mrs. Fry, and had a part in that philanthropic movement which was destined, ere long, to bring about so momentous a change in the ideas of the classes and the condition of the masses. Thus, thanks to her aunt (who was a notable woman), Miriam had not merely been well educated in the ordinary acceptation of the term, but taught, both by precept and example, to love her neighbour in that higher sense of which she had spoken to her uncle.

CHAPTER IX.

IN LOVE.

SUNDAY was an easy time at the apprentice house, and disorder ruled the roast. The apprentices were allowed to rise pretty much when they liked, and breakfast as it pleased them—always on condition that if the porridge was cold, or the "first-downs" had eaten more than their fair shares of bread, the "last-downs" should not grumble—and Dick and Betty did not begin "siding up" until the clock went twelve.

When Robin returned, several of the apprentices of both sexes, mostly half dressed, were seated at the table, eating, gossipping, and making coarse jokes; others were washing themselves at the pump, and a lot of lads and lasses, who had risen betimes, were playing a noisy game of "blackthorn, new milk, and barleycorn" in the factory yard. On one side of the fireplace sat Dick, in his shirt-sleeves, smoking a long pipe, his braces about his heels, and a week's growth of grizzly stubble on his cheeks and chin. On the other side sat Betty, also smoking a long pipe, her cap awry, her hair tousled, and her face unwashed.

"Well, how have you gone on? Did you persuade him?" asked Dick.

"No, I didn't. . ."

"I towd you so, but you wouldn't heed me. I know Owd Bob, mon. I knowed him when he wor a lad."

"I did not persuade him, but Miss Ruberry did."

"What! And is the doctor coming, then?"

"Yes. Gib has gone for him. Miss Ruberry is also coming to see Harney and inspect the house."

A live shell dropping from the ceiling, or a living snake coming down the chimney, could scarce have caused a greater sensation. Dick stopped smoking and stared in · open-mouthed astonishment. Betty let her pipe fall on the hearthstone, and sprang to her feet.

" Say that ageean—say that ageean, if you dare ! " she exclaimed.

Robin laughed and said it again.

" Bithmon ! there's nowt to laugh at. Aw these fine folk coming—and hor fresh fro' London—and me i' this state, and th' hoyle upside down ! "

" And me not shaved, and my razzur that dull as it wouldn't shave a scalded pig, not if you lathered it wi' sainted soap. Where's my holiday shirt, Betty ? "

" How do I know ? Thou mun find it for thysel'. But first of aw go and waken th' lads, and tell 'em as if they aren't down to breakfast i' five minutes they'll have to go wi' empty bellies till dinner-time. Tak' thy whip. I'll look after th' lasses and get some on 'em to side up a bit, while I get mysel' tidied and don my holiday cap and bedgown.

I never knew such a thing i' my life. What
has put it into her yed, I wonder? How
soon will hoo be here, thinken yo'? In about
an hour! Well, we can get sided up a little
bit afore then. But I wish I had known last
neet—I do that."

By this time Dick was up-stairs, cracking
his whip, and threatening the direst vengeance on all who did not "look sharp"; and
the loiterers, mortally afraid of missing their
breakfast, were coming down-stairs almost
heels over head, many of them with their
garments in their hands, or under their
arms.

A few minutes later the "siding up" began
in real earnest, and by the time Miriam
appeared, the place, though far from being
clean, was less dirty and disorderly than
Robin had yet seen it. As, moreover, Dick
had banished to a remote corner of the factory
yard all who did not possess something like
Sunday clothes, the apprentices who remained
looked almost respectable, and having promised to administer "a d—— good hiding"

to any who misconducted themselves, he had
every reason to believe that they would
"behave dacent."

Miriam was accompanied by her father
and her uncle, who had not been without
misgivings as to the condition in which they
should find things—for the brothers were
beginning to have a dim perception of the
fact that the apprentices had possibly a right
to expect something more at their hands than
shelter and porridge. It was, therefore,
with a sense of relief that they saw that
Dick and Betty had turned the short time
at their disposal to good account, and put
the place into some sort of order. Nevertheless, when Miriam entered the "living"
room, she could hardly repress an exclamation
of dismay. The blackened ceiling, barred
windows, rude furniture, and greasy floor;
the bold looks of some of the girls, the evil
countenances of some of the boys—a consider-
able proportion of whom were of the lowest
type of London Arab—their pale unwhole-
some faces and stunted forms, gave her a

sense of pained surprise, followed by a feeling
of repulsion and disgust.

"How is that poor boy?" she asked, after
the "masters" had exchanged greetings with
Dick and Betty. "Let us go and see him."

Whereupon the party went up-stairs, and
Robin, though uninvited, followed them.

Harney was tossing about in his narrow
crib, moaning, and seemingly in great pain.

"This is no place for a sick child," said
Miriam, regarding with a shudder the grim
array of "coffins" and their dirty counter-
panes and pillows. "The very sight and
smell of it are enough to make anybody ill."

"Nay, nay; that's going too far," remon-
strated her father. "It is not a bad place
for an apprentice house bedroom. We have
not much sickness, and it's only now and
then as one dies. I don't think there has
been a death among them for ever so long.
Has there, Robert?"

"Not for nearly a month," returned Robert,
complacently; but he took care not to mention that two had died the month before.

"Besides," continued Mr. Ruberry, "where else can we put him? This is the only lads' room we have."

"We might take him home, and . . ."

"Take a sick factory lad to our house! Nay, by Heaven!" interrupted Mr. Ruberry, passionately. "What will you propose next, I wonder?"

Miriam, perceiving that her father was really angry, and that her persistence might do more harm than good, wisely made no reply. This gave him time to cool; and thinking that his language had, perhaps, been a little more violent than was either seemly or necessary, he urged, as a conclusive reason against her proposal, that if they took Harney into their own house, they could not consistently refuse to do as much for other sick apprentices—"and that would not do at all, you know."

"Of course not. But wouldn't it be possible to convert one of the cottages into a sort of hospital?"

"I don't think your uncle would agree

to that. We are short of cottages, as it is; and then, consider the expense!"

Miriam was prevented from replying by the arrival of the doctor, a little man with a big paunch, a pink nose, and a peremptory manner. His first proceeding was to order the visitors to the other end of the room.

"Leave him to me and Betty," he said. "She knows what to do. I have had her as helper before. I must examine these fingers."

"Do you sleep here, Mr. Nelson?" asked Miriam, as they moved away.

"Yes, I sleep in the coffin next to Harney's."

"Coffin! Why do you call them coffins?"

"Partly, I think, because the bunks, being, as you see, narrow and painted black, are not unlike coffins; and there is a tradition among the apprentices that somebody has died in every one of them."

"How dreadful! I wonder how you can bear to sleep here. It reminds me of Newgate."

"Newgate! But you were never in New-gate, Miss Ruberry?"

"I went several times with Mrs. Brans-combe and Mrs. Fry to see the female prisoners, and read to them. Were you ever there?"

"Yes, I have been in Newgate," answered Robin, with a deep sigh, as he thought of his mother.

"You have been in Newgate, Nelson! What for?" asked Old Bob, who, though engaged in conversation with his brother, had overheard Robin's answer.

"I went with Mr. Bartlett to see—" (hesitating)—"to see a prisoner in whom he took an interest."

"Who? What prisoner?"

Miriam, seeing that Robin looked embarrassed, came to the rescue.

"Did you not hear him say, uncle, that it was a prisoner in whom Mr. Bartlett took an interest? Mrs. Branscombe took an interest in several prisoners. There was one I remember particularly—a poor creature under

sentence of death, and she had a little boy.
I wonder what became of him? But the
prisoners are much better treated now."

"Humph! I did not know as young folks
were allowed to visit prisoners in Newgate,
unless they belonged to 'em in some way;"
and with a curious glance at Robin, who was
pale and all in a tremble, he resumed his
conversation with Ben.

"I am not surprised that you are over-
come with the recollection of the scenes you
witnessed in Newgate," said Miriam, softly.
"They are terrible. Sometimes they haunt
my dreams."

"And mine. Newgate is associated with
the most terrible event in my life. The
prisoner I went to see . . ."

And then, remembering himself, he stopped
short. Miriam's manner was so sympathetic,
her voice so low and sweet, that he had been
on the point of telling her all. But if she
knew who the prisoner was, and that his
mother died in the dock of the Old Bailey!
. . . What her uncle and others would think

and say, if they knew, was only too evident, and rendered the strict guarding of his secret more imperative than ever.

Miriam, surprised and curious, but too courteous and kind-hearted to press Robin with questions, hesitated what to say, or whether to say anything, and there ensued a pause which was only saved from becoming embarrassing by an exclamation from the doctor.

"Will you come hither a moment, Mr. Ruberry, if you please?" he said; whereupon all returned to the bedside. "Look at these fingers! These are no mere flesh wounds. The bones are broken. Why was I not sent for at once? How can you expect a surgeon to treat a case successfully when it has been well-nigh ruined by one of your cursed factory bone-setters? For the child's sake, I will try to save his hand; but"—lowering his voice that Harney might not hear—"it is a very serious case, and I should not be surprised if it were to end in lockjaw or blood-poisoning. A thousand pities I was not called in sooner!"

And then, while the poor child writhed and sobbed with pain, the doctor bound up and spelked his maimed fingers.

Robin and Miriam exchanged pitying glances.

"I knew how it would be when we sent for him," said Rob to Ben, in an angry whisper. "If th' lad gets better, it will be all his cleverness; if he dees, it will be all our fault. It comes of heeding Miriam. You are too soft, Ben."

"So are you. It was your doing as much as mine. And, to tell the truth, I think it would have been just as well if we had sent for him sooner."

Old Bob made no reply, but he looked as black as thunder.

"Can anything more be done for the poor boy, Dr. Radley?" inquired Miriam.

"Nay, I think everything has been done for him that can be done—for the present. I have brought a soothing mixture, which Betty can give him as directed. He will have a good deal of pain, I dare say. It is

a serious case, but I hope we shall be able
to save his life and avoid amputation. I will
come again to-morrow. Good-day to you
all;" and with that the doctor went his
way.

After saying a few kind words to Harney,
Miriam asked Robin whether he was going to
church.

"Yes—no—I think not," was the rather
confused answer. "I should like, but somebody had better sit with Harney—poor little
chap! He might want something, and Betty
has the house to look after. I think I will
stay here."

"By all means do so," she said, with glistening eyes. "And could you run up this evening and let us know how he is? I should
be so glad."

"Certainly, Miss Ruberry. I will do so
with pleasure."

He was going to say "with all my heart,"
but checked himself in time.

"Who is she, Nelson?" asked Harney
when his visitors were gone.

" Miss Ruberry — Mr. Ruberry's only daughter."

"Did you hear how she spoke to me? Such a sweet voice! She makes me think of my sister that died."

"And such a sweet face! She makes me think of my mother."

She made him think of his mother. In many respects Miriam strangely resembled her. Both had the same violet eyes, dark hair, oval face, and fair skin, the same sweet voice and sympathetic manner. At the same age, he thought, his mother must have been still more like Mr. Ruberry's daughter. Or was it that the resemblance existed only in his imagination, and that he ascribed to one the qualities of the other? For all unconsciously, and without, as yet, even faintly realizing the fact, Robin had fallen in love with Miriam. Nor was there in this anything very surprising. Most lads of eighteen or nineteen have either been in love, or fancied they were— probably more than once. With Robin, however, it was no case of mere calf-love. To

love somebody was a necessity of his nature.
He had worshipped his mother as a superior
being; he had loved Mr. Bartlett as a second
father; and the love which he had cherished
for them, or which, in happier circumstances,
he might have cherished for brothers and
sister, he gave to Miriam. So far from holding herself coldly aloof (as, having regard to
their relative positions, she well might have
done), she had spoken to him kindly, and
treated him with a delicate consideration
which was as gratifying as it was unexpected.
And then her manner was so gracious, her
face so fair—how could he help loving her?
He more than loved her—he worshipped her;
she was enthroned in his heart. For the mere
pleasure of being near her, and sometimes
seeing her and speaking with her, he would
be content to remain at Birch Dene for years
—always. Yet in this love of Robin for
Miriam there was nothing earthly or sexual,
whatever it might subsequently become.
Rather was it the affection of a brother for a
favourite sister grafted on the passion of a

mediæval knight for an ideal lady-love. The thought that he should ever avow his love had not so much as crossed his mind. So to conduct himself as to win her approval and secure her friendship was all—for the present —to which he aspired.

To this end he had already done an act of severe self-denial. Nothing would have gratified him more than to follow Miriam to church, and get an occasional glimpse at her over the pew backs, but he felt that it would please her better if he stayed with Harney. It may be, also, that he was moved by a generous impulse. Virtue and love went together, as they always should. And he did not go unrewarded. She had smiled approval of his resolve, and asked him to go up to Oaken Cleugh in the evening. That would be better than seeing her at church.

"Why cannot you speak, Nelson? What are you thinking about?" said Harney, querulously.

"Thinking about! Nothing—that is, nothing very particular," said Robin, wakening up from his day-dream. "How do you feel now? Can I do anything for you?"

"My hand does so ache, Nelson, right up to the shoulder. But I think it will be a little better soon. They say you are a scholar. If you could read something out of a tale book, it might make the pain easier to bear."

"Of course I can. Let me see! What shall I read you? Did you ever hear of *Ali Baba and the Forty Thieves?*"

"No, Nelson. Was they hanged?"

"No, they were boiled."

"Boiled! I am sure that would be nice. Do read it, Nelson."

"I'll go and fetch the book. I shall be back in two minutes."

Robin kept his books in Betty's linen press. Among them was a copy of *The Arabian Nights*—a gift from Mr. Bartlett. Dick saw him take it, and asked what he was after. Robin told him.

"I'll go wi' you and hearken," he said.

Two or three of the apprentices, who were by, said they would also like to hearken, and all followed him up-stairs, each carrying a three-legged stool. After raising Harney's pillow, and letting him drink, Robin sat down on a rush-bottomed chair without a back—the only one in the room—and proceeded to read the story of *Ali Baba*, to which his auditors listened with rapt attention. Then, bethinking him that *The Arabian Nights* was not exactly a Sunday book (he wondered what books Miriam read on Sundays), he fetched a Bible, and by way of striking an average, read the fine Oriental story of Joseph and his brethren.

"They're both good tales," observed Dick, thoughtfully; "but I like that about them thieves best. That Morgiana wor a gradely lass—fit to turn out, hoo wor. I don't quite see, though, where hoo geet aw th' hot water. It would tak' a sight o' hot water to scawd forty thieves. It tak's five or six gallons to scawd a pig. But what a foo' that chap wor to forget th' word—'Oppen Sezme!' Onybody could mind that. 'Oppen Sezme!' Its welly same as 'Oppen, sez I!'"

"I am not so sure of that," said Robin. "It's a good deal easier to forget than to remember sometimes. I have forgotten a word which I would give a great deal to remember."

"What is it?"

"That is exactly what I want to know."

"I mean what mak' of a word is it—owt like 'Oppen Sezme?'"

"No, it's a name."

"A lass's name?"

"No, a man's name."

"Who wor he?"

"A man I knew a long time ago."

"It'll come to you one o' these days—ten to one when you're least expecting it. It is no use hosting"—[trying]—"when you've forgotten owt. There's nowt for it but to wait, and the less you think about it the better."

CHAPTER X.

"Evening" is a word of varied significa-
tion. Among common folks, who rise betimes, go early to bed, and say "good night"
before sunset, it means almost any time after
noon; while among M. P.'s, slaves of the pen,
and people of fashion, who turn night into
day, evening only begins with the dinner
hour.

Robin found this looseness of definition
useful. He had agreed to see Miriam in the
evening—an arrangement which left a good
deal to his discretion. After long thought
he came to the conclusion that he would be
none too soon if he went about four o'clock.
So at half-past three he put the finishing
touches to his toilette (with the help of a

cracked looking-glass, borrowed from Betty), and a few minutes later set out on his errand.

Meanwhile Miriam sat all alone in the drawing-room at Oaken Cleugh, reading the *Imitation of Christ*. Every now and again she would lay down her book and glance pensively into the leaf-strewn garden, where drooping dahlias and faded rose-trees betokened the coming of winter; and over the wild stretch of moorland beyond, now crimsoned with the last rays of the departing sun.

Her father and her uncle, who had dined heartily and drunk quite as much wine as was good for them, were dozing and smoking away the afternoon in the breakfast-room.

A chill sense of disappointment was beginning to creep over the girl. Birch Dene hardly differed more from London than Oaken Cleugh differed from her Aunt Branscombe's house at Clapham. There she had friends of her own age and sex, congenial society, a refined home, and the continual companionship of a woman whom she revered as a

mother and loved as a sister. Here she
despaired of finding even a potential friend.
Society was limited to the rector and his
wife—the one a lazy latitudinarian, the other
an empty-headed gossip; and, so far as
Miriam knew, there was nobody in the neighbourhood to whom she could appeal for the
sympathy for which she yearned, and the
counsel of which she already felt the need.
True, she was beloved by her father, and
loved him warmly in return; but they had
been so long separated, he was so much her
elder, their views of life differed so widely,
that it was scarcely possible there could ever
prevail between them that community of feeling and aspiration, that tender love on the
one side and trustful affection on the other,
which sometimes unite father and daughter
in the bonds of an ideal and life-long friendship. Lonely she was, and lonely she feared
she would have to remain. On the other
hand, she need neither be idle nor unhappy.
There was more than enough for her to do, as
Mrs. Branscombe had hinted there would be.

"It will be a great change for you," she had said, "and I dare say you will often get terribly homesick. But whatever you do, don't brood. Work! You will find scope enough for your energies down there—perhaps more than enough."

Her aunt spoke with knowledge, and was proving a true prophet. The management of the house and the reform of the household had so far provided Miriam with a sufficiency of occupation, and the condition of things at the factory and the farm simply appalled her. Everybody about the place drank, and nobody seemed to care. Her father and her uncle did not appear to have the faintest conception that their duty as Christians involved any concern either for the bodies or souls of those whom they employed. The mill was a contrivance for making money, regardless of the welfare or even the lives of those by whose industry its owners were enriched. . . . Those unfortunate children! The state of the apprentice house was simply shameful, the squalor of some of the cottages into which she had looked past belief. Yet what could she do? Her father she might possibly awaken to a sense of his responsibilities, but her uncle was made of less yielding stuff, and although he had so far been unexpectedly kind, she felt sure that in anything which seriously affected his pocket, or ran counter to his prejudices, he would be as hard as iron. And who was there to help her in the struggle which, unless she was content to rest with folded hands, she saw was before her? Not a soul. . . . Yes, Nelson. He was intelligent and kind-hearted, seemed anxious to please her, and would surely help her all he could. He had been very good to that poor boy. . . . How did he become an apprentice? she wondered, and why was he so strangely moved at the mention of Newgate? She did not like to ask him, yet would like to know. Her uncle had said at dinner that he believed Nelson had gone to Newgate because he could not help it—meaning that he had gone as a prisoner.

But she did not. Besides, as she well knew, there were many innocent in London's great prison. . . . No, it would not be right to question him—perhaps an opportunity . . .

While Miriam thus thought, Phœbe, the rosy-cheeked, entered the room, and announced that the object of her musings was in the hall, and would like to speak to her.

"It is about Harney. Show him in, Phœbe," she said.

When Robin appeared, with a bright blush on his face, and agreeably surprised at finding Miriam alone, she bade him be seated, and after thanking him for coming, asked how he had left "that poor boy."

Robin answered that Harney seemed easier, but also weaker, and that Betty, who was an experienced woman, and had seen many such cases, had very poor hopes of him.

"Indeed!" said Miriam, gravely. "I did not think it was so bad as that. I should be very sorry if—if he were not to get better."

"So should I. He is such a quiet, inoffensive little fellow. Not rough and foulmouthed, like most of them."

" Poor boy! Who are his friends?"

" I don't think he has any, unless I may call myself one."

" No parents?"

" I have heard him speak of a mother and a sister; but I believe both are dead. It is not often that workhouse apprentices have parents—who care anything about them."

" You mean they have been deserted."

" Yes."

"Where does Harney come from?"

" He came hither from St. Pancras Workhouse."

"And you, Mr. Nelson—you are surely not . . ."

"I am an apprentice like the others; but I was never in a workhouse in my life, Miss Ruberry."

"I beg your pardon. I should be sorry— I had no intention of hurting your feelings or asking an indiscreet question," said Miriam, reddening. "I was merely going to say that I was sure you could not be a workhouse apprentice."

Robin hesitated. Should he tell her all? He felt sure she would not betray his confidence, and it might make her his friend. But he was growing cunning, and it occurred to him that if he told her all then, there would be nothing left to tell another time; whereas if he told her merely a part, she might peradventure (her curiosity being whetted) favour him with another interview.

"Why were you so sure, Miss Ruberry?" he asked, smiling.

"For several reasons. But mainly because you have the speech and manner of an educated person."

"Yes; my dear friend and benefactor, Mr. Bartlett, gave me a good education. It is to him I owe my love of reading. I owe him everything, in fact. If he had lived, I should not be here."

"Friend! Benefactor! You have no father, then?"

"I hope so, but I am not sure."

"Not sure whether you have a father! But that is dreadful. You cannot mean that . . ."

"Oh, no; my father has not deserted me. He is not that sort of a man. He is an officer and a gentleman. We have lost each other. I don't know where he is, and he doesn't know where I am."

"But surely it is possible to find him! You could make inquiry."

"I might; but unfortunately I don't know his name. I have forgotten it."

"Forgotten your father's name! But it is not possible. You are joking, Mr. Nelson!" exclaimed Miriam, impetuously, and almost angrily.

"It is quite possible. I had a serious ill-ness—brain fever—which left me with an impaired memory. But everything has come back except my father's name, which is, of course, my own. The doctor said that would come too. If I heard it I should recognize it—just as when I heard the name of the ship on which I was born I recognized it at once."

"Born on a ship! How strange! And your mother—have you also lost her?"

"Utterly. She is dead;" and, in spite of himself, Robin's face blanched, and his voice trembled.

"What a sad story! I am very, very sorry for you, Nelson," murmured Miriam, shading her face with her hand. "I, too, have lost my mother, but, thank Heaven, my father still lives."

She was sorry for him! Tears of gratitude sprang to the lad's eyes.

"It is a terrible story, that of my mother's death," he said. "Some time, if you like, I will tell you all about it. But I should not like it to be known, even by your father or your uncle, that I am ignorant of my true name, and that I know not whether my father be alive or dead."

"Have no fear; I will keep your secret," returned Miriam earnestly. "Nothing you tell me shall go any further; and it might ease your mind to tell me more about your mother and yourself. Who knows?" — (smiling.) " Perhaps I might help you to remember your father's name and to find him."

" It is possible," said Robin, smiling in return, " though I don't quite see how. But never mind that. It would, as you say, ease my mind to tell you all, though I can never think of that time without pain, and I will . . ."

Just then the door opened, and Phœbe appeared with a pair of candles and a snuffer-tray, and Robin, looking at the clock on the mantelpiece, saw that the interview had lasted a full hour. It was time for him to go. The idea of inviting her guest to supper had crossed Miriam's mind ; but as neither of her elders was present, she thought she had better not. Nor did she ask him to prolong his visit. Her father might come in at any moment, and perhaps inquire what they had been talking about.

" Another time," she said, with one of the smiles that made her look so like his mother.

" We shall meet again before long, and I must not keep you longer from poor Harney. You will let me know in the morning how he is ? "

" If they will let me leave my work, I shall be very glad."

" I was forgetting that to-morrow is Monday. Never mind, I will send down, or come myself. Good-bye ! "

" Good-bye ! " repeated Robin, taking for a moment Miriam's proffered hand.

And then he went out into the darkness, but with a lightened heart, for he felt that he had in truth found a friend—a friend who understood him, whom he could love without stint, trust without reserve. As for the precise nature of this love, to what it might lead, or how his friendship with Miriam would be viewed by her father, he did not trouble himself in the least. He was young, and one of the privileges of youth is power to enjoy the present without misgiving, and think of the future without fear. .

But for the moment, at least, Robin's enjoyment was purely mental. It consisted in thinking about Miriam, and after the pleasant hour which he had passed with her in the drawing-room, with its red curtains, carpeted floor, and shining rosewood furniture, the apprentice house looked more uninviting than ever, and he almost shuddered as he heard the gabble of rough voices and screams of shrill laughter within.

"Here's Lord Nelson!" shouted several of the girls, as he opened the door. "Wheer have you been, Nelson? Look how smart he is! Why, he's quite a buck! That hat is th' last London cut—isn't it, Nelson? Is that a white shirt, or is it nobbut a dickey?" were among the questions addressed to him.

Then one of the lasses suggested that he had been "a-courting"—a remark which produced a shout of laughter.

Robin disdained to reply, and turned towards the staircase.

"Nay, don't get mad, and go off!" exclaimed Nanny Gorton, a pale young woman with red hair. "We only want to know wheer you've been."

"I've only been to Oaken Cleugh with a message," answered Robin curtly, "and now I'm going upstairs to see how Harney is."

"Been to Oaken Cleugh, has he? Then it's that Phœbe as he's after—hor wi' red cheeks and black een."

"Nay, Lord Nelson will have no sarvant. He'll have a factory lass—one of his own soort."

"And I know one as would be fain to have him, Nanny. Do you want a sweetheart, Nelson? You can have one for th' axing."

With an indignant gesture, Robin again turned away. It was not the first time he had been given to understand that he had made an impression on the heart of Nanny Gorton.

"Nay, you've no occasion to go. Don't get mad ageean, mon. If you don't want a sweetheart you're no waur for 't. You happen will some time, and if you do, you've nobbut to speyk—that's aw. We want you to read us that tale as you read to 'em up-stairs this morning, about a lass boiling forty thieves in

a washing mug. They mon ha' been little
'uns, I think."

"Not aw i' one mug, thou foo! There wor
forty mugs, and they worn't washing mugs
nayther," growled old Dick, who had evidently
been drinking. "Ay, read it agcean, Nelson;
it's a gradely good tale, and it'll be a good
example for th' lasses."

Robin had no particular desire to read *Ali
Baba* a second time; but knowing that
refusal would both cause disappointment and
bring him ill-will, he consented, stipulating,
however, that, before he began, he should see
Harney.

Old Betty was with him. In answer to
Robin's inquiry, she said that she did not
think he was any better.

"But you surely don't think he is any
worse?" whispered Robin. "He seems very
quiet."

"Ay, that's just it. He's a good deal too
quiet for my liking. He's been lying i' that
way, wi' his e'en shut, aw th' time, and he
hardly ever oppens his lips. I'm feared as

he's getting wayker; and it's not as if he had summat on his bones to fa' back on. He's as thin as a lath. But there's no telling; he'll happen pyke up a bit to'ard morning."

"At any rate, he isn't in pain, and that is a great blessing," said Robin; and after telling the old woman that he would return shortly, he went to keep his engagement with the people below. They found him a place of honour near the fireplace, and none listened more attentively than those who had heard the first reading. When Robin saw how much pleasure he had given, he was glad that he had complied with their request. The comments that followed the reading were many, and in some instances amusing.

"I say, lads," asked one of the older piecers —"I say, lads, who would you most like to boil in a mug, if you'd th' chance?"

"Ow'd Bob!"—"Owd Bob!" chorused a score of voices.

"Howd your noise, and don't tak' your mayster's name in name!" exclaimed Dick, angrily. "You'd like to boil Mester Robbut

in a mug, would you? What next, I wonder?
You'd happen like to boil me too?"

"Nay, there'd be no use i' that. You boil
yersel', Dick."

This sally evoked a burst of laughter—
("boiling" being a Lancashire synonym for
fuddling)—from all save the victim, whom it
put in a towering rage.

"I'll boil you!" he exclaimed, jumping up
and seizing his whip. "You shalln't have a
bit o' supper—not one on you. Be off to
bed this minute, or, bithmon, I'll flay you
wick!"

This ferocious threat was followed by an
outburst of angry protests. The lads swore,
the lasses scolded, yet though all kept beyond
the reach of Dick's whip, none showed a disposition to obey his order, and a serious attempt
to enforce it would probably have provoked
a mutiny. To be sent to bed supperless was
bad enough in any circumstances, but when
supper consisted of baked potatoes and red
herrings, as was the rule on Sunday nights,
the deprivation was more than human nature

could bear. But at the critical moment, when Dick stood at bay, whip in hand, facing the crowd of excited apprentices, and uttering curses both loud and deep, Robin succeeded in stilling the storm.

"Come, Dick," he said soothingly, "don't get angry. It was only a joke. Sit down, and I'll read you another story."

The effect was magical. Dick laid his whip aside, and beckoned the apprentices to resume their places.

"Another tale!" he said hoarsely. "Come on, then; let's have it. But I'll tell you what: If ony on 'em says owt to me about boiling, ageean—bithmon, I'll knock its yed off, let it be who it will!"

Robin then read *The First Voyage of Sindbad the Sailor*, and by the time it was finished the potatoes and herrings were smoking on the table.

When supper was over—and it did not take long in the eating—Robin went up-stairs to relieve Betty of her charge.

"He's just the same," she said, "nayther

spaykes nor stors, and scarce ever oppens his
een. I fear me he's but in a bad way. I've
gan him his physic; he'll not want no more
for two hours. You'll be going to bed to'ard
ten o'clock, I reckon?"

"I shall watch all night, or until there's
a change for the better."

"Change for the better! Well, it would
happen be as weel; he is in a bad way. I'll
look in last thing to see if you wanten owt,
and Dick 'll let you lie a bit longer i' th'
morning."

After a while the apprentices came to bed
—out of consideration for their sick com-
rade making as little noise as possible—and
were soon asleep, and the only sounds to be
heard in the room were deep breathings and
an occasional snore. Robin sat on the old
rush-bottomed chair; and on a three-legged
stool, which served as a table, were placed a
candlestick, a bottle of medicine, a broken
wine-glass, and an iron spoon. The candle
guttered, for the place was draughty, and as
the house did not boast a pair of snuffers,

Robin had to do the snuffing with his fingers. It was, moreover, a "dip" of indifferent quality, and gave a dim, uncertain, and almost ghastly light. When Robin wanted to look at Harney, he had to hold it over his head. Now and then he asked the poor child in a whisper how he felt, but as often as not received no answer.

And so the hours wore on.

The time and the circumstances were propitious for thought; and Robin did think, or rather dream, in a fitful, erratic fashion. He thought about his past life, his mother, Bartlett, Major Dene, very little about his father, and a great deal about Miriam, whom he pictured as he last saw her in the cosy drawing-room, with her comely face and winsome smile, her gray silk dress, the rose at her breast, which matched so well with the damask of her cheek, and in imagination heard again her sympathetic, sweet-toned voice, and felt once more the soft pressure of her hand.

Betty, coming with another candle, roused

him to a sense of the present and his duties
as nurse. The candle came none too soon;
the old one was nearly burnt out, and the
brown paper with which it was packed nearly
in a blaze.

"There!" exclaimed Betty, planting the
new candle in the molten remains of its
predecessor. "That'll last you an hour or
two, and here's two more ageean when it's
done. How is he?"

"There's no difference. He has not spoken
for a long time."

"Let's look!" and the old woman held
the candle over Harney's head. Her experienced eyes detected a change which Robin
had not perceived.

"I'se stop wi' you," she whispered; and
with that she put the candlestick and other
things at the foot of the bed, and herself on
the three-legged stool.

"There isn't the least need, Betty. You
go to bed. I'll watch."

"Howd your noise! We shall nayther on
us ha' to watch so long."

"What for?"

"He's deeing; that's what for."

"Nonsense, Betty! He has been like that all the time."

"Wait, and you'll see."

Robin said no more, but he bitterly reproached himself for letting his thoughts wander so far from the poor child whose life, though he knew it not, was ebbing away.

A little later Harney opened his eyes.

"Who's that?" he murmured, in an almost inaudible whisper.

"Me — Nelson and Betty," said Robin, bending over him.

"Where are the others?"

"In bed, asleep."

"And you are keeping me company! You've been very good to me, Nelson. . . . I say, Nelson."

"Yes, Harney."

"We came from London together, didn't we?"

"Yes, dear boy, we did."

"You and me and the others. But I shall never go back to London. I've had a dream, Nelson, and I'm going to my mother and Mary. . . . I say, Nelson."

"Yes, Harney,"

"You've been very kind—kinder than anybody else. Will you kiss me?"

Robin pressed his lips on the child's pale brow, already damp with the dew of death.

"You'll—you'll think sometimes of little Harney—won't you, Nelson?"

"As long as I live I'll think of you."

"Put your arm round me and raise me up. I—I feel faint."

Robin raised him up tenderly, and laid the dying lad's head on his shoulder.

"The candle burns dim," whispered Harney. "Bring it nearer, please."

Betty, with a significant glance at Robin, brought it nearer.

Then the child made as if he would pick something from the coverlet of the bed and

the air with the forefinger and thumb of
his unwounded hand. While this was going
on, Betty, thinking to make a better light,
tried to snuff the candle, and in her agitation
snuffed it out.

"I mun go down-stairs and leet it at
th' fire," she said. "I'll be back directly."

"Dark! Dark! Mother! Mary! I'm coming!" Robin heard the child murmur; and
then all was quiet.

When Betty returned the two were still
in the same position.

"Look!" she whispered, raising the candle.

There was no mistaking the meaning of
those glazed eyes and pallid cheeks and that
drooping jaw.

"He's goan dead," said Betty.

"God has taken him," said Robin, in a
broken voice.

"Ay, he is better off than ayther on us
now, Nelson. It mak's more than fifty as
I've seen dee i' this 'ere house, and I've
allus thowt as it wor th' best thing as could

happen to 'em. Life's most terrible hard
for poor folk. But get you off th' bed, and
I'll shut his een and tie up his face, and
when morning comes I'll get Dick to measure
him for a coffin. It's but a little 'un as he'll
need, poor lad!"

CHAPTER XI.

As Robin crossed the factory yard next morning, nearly an hour after the engine had " set on," he met Robert Ruberry.

" Is this your first appearance, Nelson ? " asked his master.

" Yes, sir."

" What the devil ! I cannot have this, you know. My time is six o'clock at th' latest ; and a piecer should be at his wheels by half-past five. You must get up as soon as you are wakened."

" So I did ; but Dick let me sleep a bit longer. I sat up till nearly midnight with Harney."

" Harney be hanged ! I cannot have work neglected for the sake of a sick apprentice."

"I am sorry if I have done wrong, sir; but the offence is one I cannot repeat, even if I would."

"Cannot repeat, even if you would! How so?"

"Poor little Harney is dead," said Robin, with difficulty keeping down a sob.

"Harney dead! Nonsense! You don't mean that?"

"I do indeed, sir. He died last night."

"Ah, well, that does make a difference, certainly. I wasn't aware you had been sitting up with him. Very sudden at the last, wasn't it?"

"It seemed so to me; but he was very ill when the doctor came, and Betty had poor hopes of him all day. Will you let Miss Ruberry know, sir? She was very anxious about him."

"Yes, I'll let her know. I'll tell her when I go up to my breakfast. That is all, I think. I shouldn't have spoken to you as I did just now if I had been aware. . . . . Be off to your work. I think Jim Rabbits wants you."

Robin went.

"Nelson!"

"Yes, sir!" said Robin, returning.

"The doctor wasn't much use, was he? Doctors seldom are, I think. It would have been just the same if we had sent for him at first."

"I don't think so," answered Robin, resolutely. "I believe that if a doctor had been called in at first, and Harney had received proper attention, he would have been alive now, and in a fair way for recovery."

"What, curse it, do you mean to say. . .?" exclaimed Old 'Bob, savagely; and then, without another word, he turned on his heel and went his way.

All this rather surprised Robin; but he had not been long enough at the place to understand its full significance. Never before had the death of an apprentice caused Robert Ruberry the slightest apparent concern. His usual remark, when anything of this sort happened, was—"Dead is he? Get him buried as soon as you can." Yet when he

learned the cause of Robin's tardiness, his
tone became almost apologetic; he had evidently an uneasy feeling that the fatal ter-
mination of Harney's illness might possibly
be ascribed to the delay in sending for a
surgeon. Moreover, instead of going to his
breakfast, he despatched a note to his brother,
saying that he was too busy to "come up,"
and asking that his breakfast might be "sent
down," adding, in a P.S.—"Miriam will be
sorry to hear that Harney died last night."

In truth, the cynical old money-spinner
was beginning to be rather afraid both of
Robin and his niece; for being neither utterly
devoid of conscience nor deliberately cruel,
he could not help seeing in their humanity
(softness he called it) an implied reproof of
his own hardness. Here was this lad, fresh
from London, refusing to give evidence against
Blincoe, stopping all night with him in the
old warehouse, sitting up with Harney, and
almost telling him (Robert Ruberry) to his
face that he had incurred the guilt of murder
by not sending sooner for a doctor! What a

piece of impudence! He had felt almost angry enough to strike him, and a few weeks earlier he probably would have struck him. Nevertheless, he could not help paying Nelson the homage of a reluctant admiration. Nelson was outspoken, and Robert Ruberry liked outspokenness; bold, and he liked boldness. He was also disposed to believe him honest (with one slight reservation), and next to passive obedience, Ruberry held honesty to be the highest virtue a youth could possess. For these reasons Robin's respect was worth having; and the idea that the young fellow probably regarded him as a tyrannical old curmudgeon was anything but soothing to his feelings.

As for his niece, he knew what she would think—how grieved she would be about Harney's death, and that, like Nelson, she would ascribe it to his neglect. Yet "Old Bob" liked Miriam so well that he was anxious both to save her pain and secure her love. Not for fifty pounds, he said to himself, would he have told her the news, and he looked forward to their next meeting with some misgiving.

And there were other causes at work which might well have tended to disturb Robert Rubery's tranquillity, and suggest grave doubts as to the wisdom of the course which he had hitherto followed. Distress was widely prevalent, political agitation active; the operatives were bitterly discontented, and almost ripe for rebellion; even his own hands were showing signs of insubordination; in several districts there had been serious rioting, the tyranny of factory masters had been violently denounced, both on the platform and in the press, and strange and startling doctrines were being openly promulgated. Only the day before had he read in a Manchester paper a protest by several leading physicians against the iniquities of the apprentice system; it was asserted that overwork was destroying annually thousands of lives, and impairing the health of a whole generation. One audacious innovator had actually gone so far as to propose an enactment for restricting the labour of women and children to eleven hours a day, and forbidding the employment of children under ten altogether !

All this, besides making Robert Ruberry uneasy and apprehensive, rendered him much more pervious to the influence of Nelson and his niece than he otherwise would have been.

The respite he gained by sending for his breakfast was of short duration. He had scarcely finished it when Miriam appeared in the office—after calling at the apprentice house, and getting from Robin and Betty a full account of Harney's death. Her face was pale, and her eyes looked reproach.

" Oh, uncle," she exclaimed, " that poor boy ! "

" Yes, it's a bad job. I—I am very sorry. You see, it did not do much good sending for the doctor, after all."

" He was sent for too late, uncle. If he had been sent for sooner, Harney would probably have been alive this moment. Both Betty and Nelson think so."

"Curse Betty and Nelson!" thought the uncle. What he said was: "They may think as they like, but you may depend upon it that it was the shock to the system that killed him. I don't believe all the doctors in Manchester could have saved him."

"Perhaps not, but we cannot be sure of that; and, at any rate, if you had called in a doctor at once we should have done our best; the issue would have been with God. It is a terrible thing to trifle with the life of a fellow creature. Don't let anything of this sort happen again, uncle; it would be too dreadful."

"I am sure I don't want anything of the sort to happen again, Miriam. It is no interest of ours for apprentices to die; they cost money, and a dead apprentice is of precious little use. What would you have us do?"

"I would have you send for a doctor at once, whenever an apprentice, or anybody else, is hurt—unless it be something very trifling——"

"Hum! But that would cost a lot of money."

"And I would have you turn two of the cottages into a hospital—one for boys, the other for girls. I have seen London hospitals, and I am sure it could easily be done. There is something horrible in the idea of the sick being in the same room as the whole—perhaps dying there like Harney; and but for Nelson, there would have been nobody with him at the last. He would have died, in the dark and alone."

"Turn two cottages into a hospital! That would be an expensive job, Miriam, and we should lose ten or twelve pounds a year in rent, to say nowt of the expense of fitting them up. The concern must not suffer, whatever happens."

To Robert Ruberry, "the concern" was a thing apart, and almost sacred. He held it his bounden duty to protect its interests and promote its prosperity by every means in his power, and was as devotedly loyal to it as some men are to a mistress, a monarch, or a cause. The factory cottages were a part of the business, and a permanent source of profit. Every man about the place, whether a benedict or a bachelor, whether he liked it or not, was compelled to take one. Several single men, who were domiciled with their parents, paid rents for not taking cottages. The idea of turning two of them into a hospital went strongly against the grain ; and when he said that the concern must not suffer, he thought he had said the last word—that the question was settled.

But Miriam, whose notions about business were somewhat hazy, failed to see the matter in the same light.

"Ten or twelve pounds a year !" she said. "What is that to a man like you? My father says you are better off than he is— that you are worth nearly a hundred thousand pounds."

"Your father talks nonsense. He's quite wrong ; I'm not worth owt like it—at least, I don't think I am—and, for Heaven's sake, keep it to yourself. If th' hands thowt I was worth half as much, they'd be striking for a rise of wages, and my life would be made a burden by folks asking for sub-scriptions."

"Will you make the hospital, then? I'll engage to obtain my father's consent,—in fact, I have done so already."

"I cannot, Miriam—I really cannot. As I said just now, the business must not suffer, whatever happens. But I'll tell you what I'll do "—(briskly, as if struck by a happy thought)—"I'll tell you what I'll do. I'll do it out of my own pocket. The rent shall be debited to my private account, and I'll be at the expense of making the alterations and maintaining a nurse—and, yes, I'll make an arrangement with Radley, give him so much a year to come whenever he's wanted, and then there'll happen be no more bother. Will that suit you?"

"Excellently well!" said Miriam, gladly, and inwardly much amused to think that, out of consideration for the concern, her uncle was assuming a charge which he might just as well have shared with her father. "Excellently well, and I thank you with all my heart."

"Is there owt else?"

"Yes; I want to speak to you about Nelson. Couldn't you put him in some better position? I am sure he is clever; he was wonderfully kind to poor Harney, and, from what Betty tells me, he is an influence for good with the other apprentices. He reads to them on Sundays, and they think all the world of him. And yet he goes about without shoes and stockings, just like a common sweeper or piecer!"

"That lad again!" exclaimed Robert Ruberry, with a laugh that sounded like a gibe. "That lad again! Everybody's wanting us to treat him different from the others. It is Nelson, and no end. But I have nowt to do wi' him. I've made him over to your father. Speak to him."

"I will, and I am sure my father will do his best. But if you would take it in hand——"

Here Miriam paused; but her uncle knew what she meant, and the implied compliment pleased him. She meant that he had more backbone than his brother—that what he willed was generally done, whereas Benjamin, though he promised freely and meant well, sometimes forgot his promises, and did not always see that his orders were carried into effect.

"Well, I'll tell you what I think of doing," he said, confidentially; "but don't let it go any further at present. As soon as Nelson has got an insight into things—and he's sharp, there's no denying that—as soon as he's got an insight into things, I mean to have him into the counting-house—he's a good scholar—and both make him useful and give him a better position. Will that please your ladyship?"

"Very much indeed, and I am sure Nelson will be grateful. But do you think it will be good for the concern?" asked Miriam, trying, not very successfully, to keep a grave countenance.

But it never occurred to Robert that any-body could be either ironical or jocular on so serious a subject, and he answered the question with all gravity.

"I do think so," he said. "If I did not, he would have to stop where he is. The concern must not suffer, whatever happens."

"Of course it must not. But if I take up your time any longer, I am afraid it will. Give me a kiss and let me go, you dear, good uncle. I thank you with all my heart; you have made me very happy."

Robert accepted the compliment, and gave the kiss with evident pleasure, and a minute afterwards Miriam was walking sedately across the yard, the observed of all observers. It was the first time within living memory that a lady had visited Birch Dene factory, and the "hands," particularly the female portion of them, crowded to the windows to have a look at "Owd Ben's lass."

"I've got well out of that," said Owd Bob to himself with a chuckle. "I feared she'd ha' cried and put her arms round my neck;

and if she had done, I could hardly have
said her nay, whatever she had asked me;
and they call me keen and hard! But
she has such winning ways, and that smile
of hers there's no resisting. . . . Gad! it's a
good thing that I had never time to get wed,
for I do believe I'm a bit soft in th' bottom.
However, there is no harm done so far. I've
promised nowt as will be detrimental to th'
business. I don't think Miriam's cottage
hospital will gain us much credit with th'
hands. They are an ungrateful lot, always
hankering after higher wages, or something
quite as unreasonable; but if it should ever
be said as we don't treat our apprentices
kindly, we can point to it as a proof to th'
contrary. The same with Nelson. We shall
be able to say that at Birch Dene, whatever
may be th' case at other factories, an apprentice as shows ability is sure to get on. And I
can make him useful. He may save his
porridge by seeing as the daily hands stick to
their work; and we want help in the counting-
house. Ben doesn't look after things as he

should, and Nutter is getting old and goamless. He did not take a single short-weight off that last invoice of cotton. And if we were to get another, he'd ten to one do no better. A known nowt is better than an unknown nowt. Ay, Nelson has shaped well, so far—there's no denying that, though it wouldn't do to tell him so; and if he is honest, and I believe he is, though there's something queer about that Newgate business —however, I'll soon find that out—if he's honest, I'll do as I promised. That will be a good thing all round. Miriam will be pleased, Ben will be pleased, and Major Dene will be pleased, and, best of all, the concern will be benefited."

As for Miriam, she had good reason to be satisfied with the turn things were taking; her uncle was proving more tractable than she expected, and though there was still much to be done, she had made a good beginning. It, moreover, pleased her greatly to think that Nelson would be put in a position better suited to his abilities and education than that of a common apprentice. She had also ascertained the limit of her power; her uncle evidently loved her, and was disposed to meet her views, but it was equally evident that he would refuse to sanction changes by which the supreme object of his affection was likely to suffer.

CHAPTER XII.

PROMOTION.

ROBERT RUBERRY was not the sort of man who lets the grass grow under his feet, and on the following day, after a talk with his brother, Robin was sent for to the counting-house, whither he went, wondering whether the summons boded him evil or good.

"You make calculations sometimes for Jim Rabbits, about speeds and that, I understand?" said Robert, rather gruffly.

"Yes, sir; but only when Jim asks me," answered Robin, thinking that helping the spinning master was going to be imputed to him as a fault.

"Oh, it's all right so long as you don't make mistakes——"

"I don't think I have, sir. If you'll ask Jim——"

"I have asked him"—(grimly)—"but never mind that. Do you know anything about bookkeeping?"

Robin had to admit that he knew very little about bookkeeping, his performances in that line having been limited to making an occasional entry in Mr. Bartlett's waste book, and checking additions in the cash book and ledger.

"Well, that's summat, and I suppose you could learn if you had the chance?"

Robin supposed he could.

"Well, you shall have the chance, and I hope you will make a good use on't." And then the younger brother told Robin what had been resolved in his behalf. He was to spend part of his time in the mill, part in the counting-house. As for his duties, they were to be rather multifarious. He was to see that the hands on daily wages did not shirk their work, and report to Mr. Robert any instances of neglect or waste which he might detect, superintend the weighing of cotton and yarn, and make himself generally useful.

"How useful you are depends entirely on yourself," said Robert. "You have got your foot on the first stave of the ladder. Climb as high as you can—only no tumbles, mind. . . . And don't you think you'd let him keep th' petty cash, Robert? He'd manage that."

"But what would Nutter say?"

"Oh, never mind Nutter; he'd have more time for other things. And you say he's very slow."

"He is; and he gets slower. Very well, let it be so then. This is it, Nelson"—(taking up a long narrow book). "I'll give you some money at the beginning of every week, and you'll have to set down everything as you pay—postage of letters, expenses to Manchester, allowance to carters, and such like. You'll soon see how it's done, and at the week end I'll balance you up."

"That is it," put in Robert. "All as you

have to do is to pay as little as you can, and set down everything as you pay. If you don't, you'll get wrong."

This was his expedient for testing Robin's integrity. It would be quite within his power to enter from time to time a few pence or even shillings without paying them. But he meant to watch him, and, as Old Bob knew, or thought he knew, from past experience, almost exactly how much the weekly petty cash should average, he would soon be able to make a pretty shrewd guess whether Robin was honest or otherwise. He had probably heard the story of the ingenuous youth who, on applying for a post as assistant-bookkeeper, and being asked how much wage he wanted, said "Thirty shillings a week," but if he might keep the petty cash he would take twenty!

The change in Robin's fortunes, albeit somewhat ungraciously announced, rejoiced him greatly, and his thanks were warmly expressed.

"Never mind thanking me; thanks are

only words. I'd liefer have deeds. Thankful is as thankful does. But if you must thank somebody, thank my niece. It is more her doing than mine."

This Robert Ruberry said because he hated sentiment and did not believe in gratitude; yet nothing he could have said would have given Robin so much pleasure. The youth forgot the ungraciousness of the uncle, and thought only of the kindness of Miriam, of which he inwardly registered a vow to be worthy.

"Yes, sir," he answered, quietly—"when shall I begin?"

"To-morrow. But you cannot go about, and come here in them things" (pointing to his greasy garments). "Have you a decent working suit?"

"No, sir."

"You'll have to get one, then. There's a ready-made shop at Toppleton; you can buy a good fustian suit and a couple of check shirts for about thirty shillings."

"Yes, sir. Shall I pay for them out of the petty cash?" asked Robin, smiling.

"He has you there, Robert!" laughed Ben. "How can th' lad find thirty shillings? We shall have to help him."

"Help him! I don't know about that. I was thinking he had happen as much laid by."

"Laid by! Did not Parson pick his pocket, and you know how much he has had since."

"Oh, ay!—I was forgetting. Well, I suppose we shall have to lend him thirty shillings then. But it must not go through th' books. If you'll find one half, I'll find t'other."

"Agreed! But hadn't we better say 'give' instead of 'lend'?" put in Benjamin, who, always more generous than his brother, happened just then to be in an exceptionally generous mood.

"Give it him! These aren't times for giving. I was thinking of stopping it at so much a week. However, he shall have the thirty shillings, and if he shapes right, we'll say no more about it. You'll have to leave th' apprentice house, Nelson."

"Where must I live, then?" asked Robin, eagerly, as a wildly absurd hope crossed his mind that it might be at Oaken Cleugh.

"With Jim Rabbits. He can find you a nook to sleep in. The concern will pay for your tooth, and your wage will be—— Three and sixpence a week, didn't we say, Ben?"

"We said five shillings."

"The deuce we did! Well, if we said so —— It's a lot of money, though. Thirteen pounds a year! But you'll have to find your own clothes, Nelson—no more loans or presents. And now"—(turning to his brother)—"hadn't you better give him the thirty shillings, and let him go to Toppleton and get what he needs this afternoon?"

Ben, nodding assent, produced the money, which Robin (having no faith in his pockets) dexterously tied in his shirt with a piece of twine.

"That's all, I think," added the other, by way of terminating the interview. "But you'll just bear in mind, Nelson, that you are still an apprentice, and willn't be your own

master till you are of age ; and if you don't
give satisfaction, you'll have to go back to
your piecing, and live in th' house again. It's
just an experiment we are trying, as I said
before, to please Miss Ruberry. She thinks
you behaved well about Harney ; but, for my
own part, I don't expect much good will come
of it."

The purpose of which observation was to prevent Robin from getting uppish and conceited,
or ascribing his promotion either to his own
merit or to Mr. Robert's kindness ; its principal effect, to convince him that he owed nothing to his masters, and everything to Miriam.

Great were the lamentations at the apprentice house when it became known that " Lord
Nelson " had received orders to change his
domicile. Betty almost cried, Dick swore that
he was the cleverest young fellow he knew,
and expressed his belief that he had a " yed
and a hoaf," and several of the maiden apprentices shed tears.

Though, as may be supposed, Robin was by
no means sorry to leave the house, he could

not help being touched by these demonstrations of affection, and he reminded his friends, by way of consolation, that flitting to Jim Rabbits' was not quite the same as going to "foreign parts," offering, at the same time, to come in and read to them on Sunday afternoons—an offer which was loudly applauded and gratefully accepted.

His fresh quarters were nothing to boast of, and had he gone thither direct from London he would probably have thought himself ill-used ; but everything is relative, and compared with the apprentice-house garret, his new bedroom seemed almost luxurious. True, it was small—about nine feet by six—and unpleasantly near the slate ; and the bed barely big enough to turn round in. On the other hand, it was clean, and he had it all to himself ; he could fix a shelf on the wall for his books, and find a place of safety for his guinea, which Betty refused to "bank" for him in her stays any longer, and which he had been sharp enough to prevent Robert Ruberry from making him invest in a suit of clothes.

Old Bob's motive for ordering him to quit the apprentice house for more expensive lodgings was, nevertheless, not quite obvious. In the first instance, Robin was rather disposed to attribute it to the influence of his adored protectress — an illusion which was, however, speedily knocked on the head by Jim Rabbits.

"What for has Mr. Robbut shifted you fro' th' 'prentice house to mine, seeing as it costs him more?" said the spinning master. "Well, he hasn't towd me, but I think it's middling plain. You're too clever for th' 'prentice house. You can read and talk, and he has happen an idea as you'll be talking and reading too much. If you took wrong ways, you might play awkerd tricks—stor up a strike, or summat o' that soort. He thinks you're safe with me—and it doesn't cost him so much more as you mut think. He beat me down most terrible. I wouldn't ha' done it, nobbut as now you are here constant I shall larn a sight faster; and when I can write and cipher, th' owd devil may go and hang hissel for owt

I care.   I shall be able to mend my shop
then."

This deliverance surprised Robin. He had
always supposed that Jim and the junior
partner were on excellent terms; but it was
evident that the latter was no better liked
by the spinning master than by anybody else.
He doubted even whether Miriam could really
like her uncle, and it pleased the young fellow
exceedingly to think that he owed her an
infinity of gratitude, and none whatever to
him, whom, rightly or wrongly, he regarded as
half tyrant, half rogue.

One of Robin's new duties was to examine
accounts, and a few days after his promotion
Robert Ruberry gave him some cotton invoices
to check.

"See as they are right added up and cast
out," he said. Whereupon Robin, going diligently to work, found an error of twenty
pounds.

"That's right!" exclaimed "Old Bob."
"Why, you've saved your wage already!
Try if you cannot find another."

Robin did find another; but on the other side—ten pounds too little charged.

"Humph!" grunted Old Bob, when he pointed this out.

"Shall I make a note of it?" asked Robin.

"Ay, you happen better had. It'll look honest. But th' next time you come across owt o' th' sort, say nowt about it. It's no business of ours to find out other folks' mistakes—when they're against us."

Robin doubted whether this was seriously meant, for albeit Mr. Robert seemed to be in earnest, there was a something in his manner which rather belied his words. At any rate, Robin continued to note all the mistakes he found, whether they were for or against; and he did wisely, Ruberry, junior, being fairly honest, according to his lights; and, had the youth acted as he suggested, he would certainly have drawn conclusions unfavourable to his personal integrity, or, as Old Bob put it tersely to himself, "If he helps me to rogue other folks, he'll help other folks to rogue me."

In one respect Robin's removal to Jim Rabbits was not to his liking. He saw less of Miriam than he would have done had he remained at the apprentice house. She called there two or three times a week, had the place thoroughly cleaned and whitewashed inside and out, talked to the girls, and took great interest in the conversion of the two adjoining cottages into a hospital. Robin seldom saw her, except at church, whither he went every Sunday morning, rain or shine. She had always a nod and a smile for him, and they exchanged an occasional greeting, but several months elapsed before he had a chance of thanking her for the propitious change in his fortunes which her influence had wrought. It happened on a Sunday. He was reading to the apprentices the story of *The Three Calendars,* when a general rustle and exclamation of surprise caused him to look up, and he found that among his hearers were Miriam and her father, who had stepped into the room almost unperceived.

"Pray go on, Nelson," she said, taking a

chair, vacated for her by one of the maiden apprentices. "We will wait till you have finished."

When the reading was over she hinted that she had something to say to him, and he followed her out of the house, Mr. Ruberry bringing up the rear.

"You read very well, Nelson, and *The Arabian Nights* is interesting; but don't you think you could find some book more suitable for the day?"

Whereupon Robin explained that he unfortunately possessed no more suitable book, and that unless he read something rather exciting, the apprentices either ceased to listen or fell asleep; that even the reading of the Bible produced this result, and they would listen neither to *Plutarch's Lives* nor Milton's poems. He observed, further, that though *The Arabian Nights* might not contain much useful information, or be religiously edifying, it excited the children's imagination, took them out of themselves, and made them forget for a while the hardship of their lot.

"I never thought of that," she said, frankly. "Yes, it must be good to make those poor children forget, sad as it is to say so; and, for my own part, I enjoy tales immensely. Still, you know, this is Sunday, and I think —— I have a good many books at home, and as you are a judge of books, why not come with me, and we will try to choose something which is edifying without being dull?"

Robin protested that nothing would please him better, and Mr. Ruberry making no objection, he went with them to Oaken Cleugh. The house was rather large of its class, containing, in auctioneer phraseology, "four entertaining rooms." One was the parlour *par excellence*, beloved by the brothers. In it they took all their meals, smoked their pipes, and spent their rare moments of leisure. The drawing-room was laid up in lavender, and the dining-room was used only on Sundays and three or four times a year, when Mr. Ruberry gave a heavy dinner to half a dozen hard-drinking friends. But Miriam changed all this. It seemed to her a waste of good things to have rooms merely for ornament, so she had them swept and warmed every day, and on a Sunday evening would tempt the brothers into the drawing-room by playing a few old-fashioned hymn tunes on her harpsichord—a present from her uncle. The fourth room was her own. Beforetime it had been called the "little room" and the "library" indifferently—albeit, until she came home, it contained nothing more literary than an empty bookcase. Now it was known as "Miss Ruberry's room"—for the word *boudoir* had not yet come into use at Birch Dene. It was a cosy little room, adjoining a small conservatory, which she filled with choice flowers. She moreover replenished the bookcase with her own literary treasures, and hung on the walls several of her water-colour sketches.

Into this room Miriam introduced Robin, and as her father, who knew nothing about books, and cared less, had betaken himself to the parlour and his pipe, the two young folks were left to themselves.

CHAPTER XIII.

AT OAKEN CLEUGH.

"Here are my books!" said Miriam. "Now let us see if we cannot find among them something—I won't say more entertaining, but better adapted for Sunday reading than *The Arabian Nights*."

"I am sure we can; but you must remember that Sunday is the only time factory folks have for reading of any sort."

This, though a sufficiently appropriate answer, had a purpose not obvious to Miriam —Robin being just then much more desirous of leading up to a conversation about themselves, and thanking her for her good offices on his behalf, than helping her to select books suitable for Sunday reading.

"That is quite true. I wish it were not.

But so far as you are concerned, you have
surely more time for reading than you had?"
said Miriam, falling straightway into the trap.

"Thanks to you, I have; and I do thank
you very much. Do not think me ungrateful
for not thanking you sooner. I had not the
chance. I shall never forget your kindness as
long as I live, Miss Ruberry."

"It is very good of you to say so, but
I don't know what I have done to deserve
so much gratitude; it was my uncle and
my father," returned Miriam, who was both
amused and surprised by the impetuosity of
the young fellow's manner, and the warmth
of his words.

"Oh, yes; they advanced me and removed
me from the apprentice house, I know; but
not because of any merit of mine. It was to
please you."

"To please me!"

"Your uncle said so. He said you had
asked him to put me in a better position,
and that I must thank you for my advance-
ment, not him."

"Yes; I believe I did suggest that he might give you a better position, but had I known that he would put it in that light, I almost think I should have held my peace," said the girl, with a smile that belied her words—for, in truth, Robin's gratitude was by no means displeasing to her. "And I am sure my uncle would not have advanced you if he had not thought you worthy of it. At any rate, he is quite satisfied with you so far—that I know."

"Does he say so?"

"He was saying only yesterday to my father that you were diligent and useful, and would soon be a great help to them; and from my uncle that is high praise."

"I am very glad. It is pleasant to know you are giving satisfaction, especially when you are trying your best. All the same, it is to you I owe the opportunity of winning your uncle's praise, and I decline to be grateful to anybody but you."

"Oh, but you must be grateful to my father and my uncle as well as to me—more than to me, for I did very little," said Miriam, with a slight blush. "But let us look at the books. What do you think of this?"

Robin answered by inquiring what she thought, and there followed a little discussion on the general subject, into which, however, neither of them put much heart, for both were thinking of something else. He wanted to continue the personal narrative, which he had left unfinished on the occasion of his previous visit, yet hesitated to resume it without being asked, and though Miriam was burning with curiosity to hear it, she equally hesitated to ask him—partly out of a feeling of delicacy, partly perhaps from another and less definable feeling.

From this embarrassment they were relieved by an opportune accident.

Robin took up at random a book, the title of which happened to be, *Where Is Your Father?* It had a religious application, but it applied in a special manner to himself.

"This might be meant for me?" said Robin, showing Miriam the book.

" So it might. How strange it is you should light on that book! Have you—I suppose you have not yet been able to think of the name of your father—your earthly father, I mean—for the title refers to our heavenly Father ? "

" I am sorry to say I have not. You said you might perhaps help me to remember it."

" Perhaps I might if I knew the whole of your story. At the same time, if you would rather not tell me, don't hesitate to say so. I should be very sorry to give you pain, and you said——"

" But I rather would, Miss Ruberry, if you would kindly let me. True, mine is a mournful story; but if I might—you said, you know, that it might ease my mind, and that you might perhaps help me to remember my father's name and my own. You have no idea what a strange feeling it is not to know your own name. May I ? "

" Of course you may. The little you told me the last time you were here interested me so much that I shall be glad to know all."

"And I will tell you all, Miss Ruberry. It were ungrateful to have any secrets from so kind a friend."

Miriam, slightly blushing, acknowledged the compliment with a gracious smile, and signing to Robin to take a seat (they had been standing near the bookcase), took one herself.

"If you are ready to begin I am ready to listen," she said, simply. "My father and uncle are in the parlour, and we are not likely to be interrupted. We can look at the books afterwards."

On this hint Robin spoke. He told Miriam all that the reader knows, and something more, for he began with his earliest recollections—gave an account of his life in Hampshire and a dimly-remembered visit of his father; of the summons to meet him in London, and the journey thither; of the gradual waning of his mother's hopes; of their deepening poverty and growing despair; of their expulsion from their lodgings; of the

arrest, the trial, the terrible scene in the Old
Bailey, and everything that had since befallen
him.

To this strange eventful history the young
girl listened with intense interest and undis-
guised sympathy; and when Robin, in a voice
broken with emotion, told of his mother's
imprisonment, and described her death and
his own illness and despair, Miriam bent her
head and wept.

So much was she moved, indeed, that it
was some minutes after Robin had finished
his tale before her feelings would permit her
to speak.

"I never heard the like!" she said at
length. "Poor boy! Poor mother! If I
had not seen with my own eyes—if I had not
visited Newgate, I would not believe that
men could be so cruel. Yet I am sure your
story is true. But the pity of it—the pity of
it! . . . Just now you called me your friend.
You did right; I am your friend. Look on
me as a sister, and I will help you to find
your father and think of his name. We must

find him. Your heavenly Father, who has so wonderfully protected you, will open a way. Be sure that he has led you here to Birch Dene for some wise end, though it is still hidden from us."

"Do you really mean that—that you will let me call you sister—Miriam, and that you will call me brother—Robin?" demanded the young fellow, with glistening eyes and perhaps more impetuosity than the occasion absolutely required.

"Yes," answered Miriam, dubiously, after a moment's consideration; for she had not expected to be so promptly taken at her word —"yes, I think so; for if I am as your sister, you are of course as my brother. But only between ourselves. My father and my uncle might possibly not view the matter as we would like them."

"That is what I mean—only between ourselves. I would not mention it to anybody for the world. It is happiness enough for me to think of you as my sister, and to know that you regard me as your brother."

"I think we had better continue our examination of the books," said Miriam, dryly, at the same time rising from her chair and suiting the action to the word.

Though Robin was quite at a loss to understand what this sudden change of mood might portend, he felt that he had somehow put his foot in it, and with an abashed look, silently resumed his inspection of the bookcase.

And perhaps it was as well he did, for shortly afterwards the door was unceremoniously thrown open, and Mr. Ruberry, fragrant with tobacco smoke, entered the room.

"What! Among your books yet?" he exclaimed, good-naturedly. "I never saw owt like it. It might be a big business. How soon will you have done?"

"I think we have done now, father," returned Miriam, quietly. "The work of selection has been— just a little difficult. If you take these four, Nelson, I dare say they will be enough for the present. Use those you think the most suitable, and when you want more, you can come again. I suppose you will want your tea soon, father? I will see after it myself. I have let Polly and Phœbe go out, and there is only Margaret in the kitchen."

" Well, when it's ready for us, I dare say we shall be ready for it. Will you be playing on your harpsichord after tea, think you?"

" Certainly, father, I shall be very glad— unless you and uncle prefer your pipes."

" Nay, we'll have some music first; th' pipes will do later on. Are you going, Nelson?"

" Yes, sir. I think it is about time,' answered Robin, as he tied a piece of string round his books. " Can I do anything more for you, Miss Ruberry?"

" Thank you, I am not aware that you can —at present. But there is no need for you to go just yet. Tea will be on shortly. He might stay and have a cup—mightn't he, father?"

" Ay, let him stay if he likes," was the not very gracious response.

" Would you like to stay and take tea with us, Nelson?" added Miriam, kindly, with a glance which, as he thought, meant that it would please her if he did, and which made amends for his recent rebuff. So he thanked her and said "Yes." This matter being settled she betook herself to the kitchen, and on Mr. Ruberry's invitation Robin accompanied him to the parlour, where they found "Old Bob" sitting on a rocking-chair by the fireside, wearing his Sunday spectacles and deep in a newspaper. Working days being too precious for such trivialities, he always got up the news of the previous week on the Sunday afternoon; and, when he had not been to church in the morning, squared the account by reading a chapter in the Bible as well.

It was the first time Robin had seen the junior partner taking his ease, and he looked so different from his usual self that it needed an effort to believe him to be the same man. His face had lost, for the nonce, its hard cynical expression, his lips wore something like a smile, his manner was mild, and his voice subdued. Robin was at first disposed to ascribe the metamorphosis to Miriam's influence, and to this cause it may have been in some measure due; but he learnt afterwards that Robert Ruberry was always affable at home, and as popular with the maids as he was unpopular with the hands. It was the difference between a general at the head of an army in the field and in the bosom of his family.

"Oh, it is you, is it, Nelson?" he said, looking up. "Willn't you take a chair? How's th' petty cash going on?"—smiling.

"It is hardly for me to say, sir. But I think I have kept it right so far."

"Ay, has he," put in Mr. Ruberry, heartily; "and what is more, he keeps it down. I've balanced him up regular, and for the time as he has had it, th' weekly average is fifteen shillings less than it used to be."

"And that is how long?"

"Going in six months."

"That's a fair average. One week does not amount to much, but five or six months tells a tale. Let's see! Twenty times fifteen makes

fifteen pounds. That's a fine saving. Keep
it up, Nelson—keep it up! Always do your
best for your employers, and they'll do their
best for you, to say nowt of the satisfaction it'll
be to your conscience. See how many folks
we find in porridge every week! Yet I don't
believe as there's half a dozen on th' ground as
ever think how much they owe us, and if it
wasn't for our capital and the way we look
after things they'd have to clem [starve].
They think more of robbing us—and they
do, too."

And as if the mere idea of ingratitude so
base had touched him to the quick, the
speaker's face darkened, and his voice trembled
with sorrowful indignation.

"Robbing you!" exclaimed Robin, moved
in turn to indignation by this sweeping impu-
tation on the characters of the hard-working,
ill-paid factory hands of Birch Dene. "Hardly
that, Mr. Robert. How can they rob you?"

"Oh, I don't mean as they actually carry
things off th' ground. They are too well
looked after for that. I mean as they idle

away a good deal of their time. When I see
a chap idling, I feel it just as much as if he
had his hand in my pocket."

"But most of them are on piecework, and
if they are idle, the loss is their own, you
know."

"And isn't it ours too? Aren't the fixed
expenses—rates and taxes, interest of money,
wear and tear of machinery—aren't they just
the same, whether we turn out owt or nowt?
And if we don't turn out a good deal, we shall
soon be ruined."

"Business again, uncle!" said Miriam, who
just then came in. "I thought you did not
let it trouble you on Sundays?"

"No more I do, except when summat
brings it to my mind. Nelson here seemed
to think that hands on piecework can waste
their time without th' concern suffering, and I
was merely explaining that fixed expenses are
just th' same, whether we turn out much or
little."

"What deplorable ignorance! I hope he
has grasped the point. Have you, Nelson?"

"I think I have.   All the same——"

"Never mind all the same.   If you say any more, uncle will consider it his duty to make another explanation, and we shall be talking business all the evening."

"That is right, Miriam—we shall," observed her father.   "Ay, let's talk about summat else.   What do you think them bullocks made, Robert, as I sent to Preston?"

"Oh, it has to be bullocks, has it?" laughed Miriam.   "I think I would rather have a discussion on fixed expenses than a talk about bullocks."

"Why, God bless me! what would the lass have?" exclaimed Mr. Ruberry, with a bewildered look.   "Neither business nor bullocks!   What must it be, then?"

"Uncle has been reading the papers all afternoon.   Has he no news to tell us? Perhaps he will oblige us by starting a subject which has no relation either to bullocks or fixed expenses?"

"That is a good idea.   Ay, do, Robert," interposed his brother.   "I never read owt but th' market reports and cock-fights myself. You read everything. Is there owt going on ?"

"Lots. There has been a mill between Conkey Jim and the Hammersmith Pet. Two or three of the Royal princes were there, and ever so many noblemen. They say as the Prince Regent backed th' Pet to th' tune of a thousand pounds. If he did, he lost it, for th' Pet came off second best. Then there was a bull bait last week at Leeds, and th' bull broke loose and tossed six or seven folks over his head, and as many more were thrown down and trodden to death, and th' Carlisle mail coach has been robbed by two highwaymen between Garstang and Lancaster——"

"What! I thought all the highwaymen had been wiped out."

"It doesn't seem so ; and, really, what wi' robbery, riot, and murder, I don't know what th' country is coming to. However, I'm glad to see that th' authorities are acting with vigour. Seven men and two women have been sentenced to death at Lancaster—two of 'em for stealing pieces off a croft—and a meeting of weavers at Burnley to petition for reform has been dispersed and th' ringleaders arrested. And serve 'em right too! I'd transport every one of 'em. What do they know about politics? Let 'em stop at home and mind their looms, and be contented with that state of life as God has given 'em. I'm content; why shouldn't they be?—and I work as hard as anybody. To hear some folks talk, we might be the most down-trodden and ill-used people as is, yet I'll be bound to say as that there isn't anywhere a better governed or a happier country than this."

"Although, what with robbery, murder, and riot, you don't know what it is coming to, Uncle Robert," observed Miriam, with an amused smile.

"Did I say so? I didn't mean; I mean I did not—you take one up so sharp, Miriam," he stammered, after a stare of annoyance and surprise. "And if things are not quite what they should be, it isn't the fault of the Government or the laws. While the war lasted the

Jacobites were never tired of prating about peace and plenty. Well, we've got peace, and now plenty seems farther off than ever. Shows what fools they are."

"That reminds me — talking of peace, I mean—that reminds me of Major Dene," put in Mr. Ruberry—"Colonel Dene, I should say; he's got promoted, you know. Is there owt about him in th' papers you have been reading?"

"In what way? There's been no *Gazette* lately, has there?"

"Don't you know? I thought I'd told you. His regiment forms part of the army of occupation in France. He had been on furlough since Waterloo—owing to his wound—and when he was promoted to the colonelcy, had to go off at a minute's notice. That's why Mrs. Dene did not call on Miriam; she went with him. I thought the regiment might have been ordered home. When it is he means to retire on half-pay, and settle down at Dene Hall for good. He doesn't think there's any likelihood of another war for a long time, and he would rather lead the life of a country gentleman, and look after his estates, than waste his time in country quarters. That's what he told me."

" He'll ten to one be back soon, then ? "

" He'll not leave the regiment before it leaves France, and that mayn't be for twelve or eighteen months; at least, so th' steward was saying t'other day."

" Well, he hasn't been at home much since he came into th' property, has he ? "

" About six or seven months in as many years. He has seen a lot of service, Colonel Dene has."

" Colonel Dene was old Mr. Dene's nephew —wasn't he, father ? " asked Miriam. " I just remember him driving about in a low carriage, with a pair of piebald ponies. He always gave me a kindly nod."

" Ay, a fine old English gentleman was Mr. Dene. Uncommonly fond of cock-fighting he was ; never had less than a hundred brace of game birds in prime condition. Many a main I've seen 'em fight, and before he got so gouty he'd ride fifty miles any day to see a bull or a bear bait. And the cellar of port wine he kept! Nobody had to dine with Mr. Dene as couldn't carry two or three bottles of it away under his belt; and he made a rule of getting drunk at least once a week. He had a head, he had. I never saw his like; there's no such heads now-a-days "—(sighing).

"What a pleasant old gentleman! Major —I mean Colonel—Dene doesn't seem to resemble him much."

" Not a bit. He hasn't a head worth a row of pins. Why, he drinks claret, and I've heard of him saying as he thought cock-fighting and bull-baiting cruel sports. But then there was not much kinship between them."

"I thought old Mr. Dene was the colonel's uncle."

"Not quite. They came off th' same stock, however. Th' colonel's mother was own niece to Mr. Dene's half-brother. Th' old squire's had nephews of his own, and all of 'em expected to get th' property; and they say as

he left it to th' colonel just to spite 'em all.
And a good job too; them nephews were a
rare lot of wastrels."

"He had to change his name, hadn't he?"
put in Robert.

"Ay, that was the condition, I believe."

"Indeed! I did not know that," said
Miriam, in some surprise. "What used the
Colonel's name to be?"

"I've clean forgotten, lass. It's a long
time since I heard it, and I've never known
him as owt but Colonel Dene. What was it,
Robert?"

"Nay, I can't tell. I've quite enough to
do to mind my own business, without keeping
other folks' names i' my head, as I haven't
heard for years, and care nowt about. And
what does it matter? We know who he is
now."

At this point the door was furtively pushed
open a few inches, and Margaret (who was
given to shyness) informed her young mistress
in a stage whisper that "tay was ready."

Thereupon all filed into the dining-room,

and Robin had the felicity of sitting at Miriam's left hand.

The tea-service was of exquisite old china, as fine and as transparent as a sea-shell, and the teapot (which had belonged to her grandmother) was something to live up to, and would have made a modern collector die of envy. But there were no plates—wooden platters for tea and breakfast being still the fashion at Oaken Cleugh. The bread was served up in slices of wafer-like thinness, well buttered, and there were muffins, crumpets, boiled eggs, and ham collops in almost lavish profusion. The beverage which gave its name to the repast was strong and fragrant, which, seeing that tea at that time cost from five to six shillings a pound, was perhaps more than might have been expected. But it was a tradition at Oaken Cleugh to have everything of the best, especially in the way of eatables and drinkables.

After tea the party adjourned to the drawing-room, and Miriam, seating herself at the harpsichord, sang and played, chiefly old-fashioned hymn tunes. Robin, who stood by with beaming face, turned over the leaves of her music-book. The improvised concert concluded with the singing of the doxology, in which " Old Bob " joined with seeming fervour, and in a somewhat harsh, yet not untuneful voice. The young fellow would fain have lingered a little longer; but when Mr. Ruberry said something about whisky and water, and its being nearly bedtime, he took it as a hint that he had outstayed his welcome, and after bidding the brothers and Miriam good-night, and thanking them for their hospitality, he went his way.

CHAPTER XIV.

" WHAT do you think of this reading and going on, Robert ? " asked Benjamin of his brother, as they were sipping their grog in the parlour, after Robin's departure.

" Well, I cannot say as I particularly like it. The less apprentices know about books and such like the better, in my opinion. But what can you do? It pleases Miriam, and happen does not do so much harm, after all. It isn't as if the apprentices were learning to read—that wouldn't do at all. They'd be lazier and more discontented than they are now. But there's one thing you'll have to mind. You'll have to take care as them two doesn't get too thick."

" Too thick! What do you mean ? "

"What I say. What folks generally do mean when they talk about lasses and lads getting too thick."

"But—you don't know what you are talking about, Robert!" exclaimed Mr. Ruberry, excitedly. "It is quite impossible. You forget, I think, that Miriam is my daughter, and Nelson nowt but a common parish apprentice."

"And she's a lass and he's a lad, and when lasses and lads get together, they do sometimes get too thick. However, it's nowt to me. I only thought . . ."

"It's absurd—impossible!" interrupted the other, angrily. "I wonder at you, Robert! You are too suspicious—too suspicious by half."

"Well, I happen am; but Miriam is very young, remember, and when lasses are at that age . . ."

"What does an old bachelor like you know about lasses?"

"Humph! There's many an old bachelor knows more about lasses than married men do," rejoined Robert, with a cynical laugh. "That's the main reason why they keep single."

"It's perfectly ridiculous, I tell you!" said Ben, now quite in a fume. "Such an idea could not possibly enter Miriam's head. She's as good as gold!"

"You're right there, she is, but very inexperienced and without a mother; and Nelson is a good-looking young fellow, and he knows about books, and can talk gradely English."

"What by that? He's nowt but a factory lad, and she'd never think, and he'd never dare . . . It's all nonsense! I mean Miriam to marry a man of birth and breeding, and what I tell her she'll do."

Robert Ruberry leaned back in his chair and laughed heartily.

"You think so, do you?" he exclaimed. "Well, I don't reckon to be much of a prophet, but I'll prophesy one thing: When th' time comes she'll please herself, not you. Mark me if she doesn't. All th' same, I shall

be fain if she does wed a highflyer—what
you call a man of birth and breeding—but
you may take your davy as she willn't let
you pick and choose for her. Miriam isn't
a lass of that sort, and if you let on as you're
expecting owt of th' sort, it will just set her
against it. However, it's nowt to me. She's
your daughter, not mine. I only thought as
I would just drop you a bit of a hint."

"A bit of a hint! I call it a d—— broad
hint," growled Mr. Ruberry, as he mixed
himself a glass of punch. "And I don't
know as I want any hints. I dare say I
can see as far into a stone wall as anybody
else."

Robert smiled sardonically, as if he was
not quite sure about it. Ben, however, made
no further remark, but went on silently smoking, as if his thoughts were too big for
words.

Although Mr. Ruberry resented his brother's
interference in his family concerns, and affected
to despise his warnings, they made their
mark, and the longer he pondered them the

less he liked him. The contingency suggested by Robert was at least possible, and
albeit he tried to persuade himself that Miriam
" would have more sense," and Nelson " would
never have the impudence to think of such
a thing," the result of his musings (extend-
ing intermittently over several days) was a
resolve to forbid him the house, and put
Miriam on her guard.

"Have you seen owt of Nelson lately?"
he asked her, with assumed indifference, as
they sat one evening at tea. "You said
something about him having some more books,
didn't you?"

"It is hardly possible he can have read
those he took already. It was only last
Sunday but one that he was here."

"So you don't think he's likely to be
coming again just yet?"

"Unless he finds the books unsuitable."

"And he very likely will."

"What makes you think that, father?"

"For th' sake of coming here—and getting
asked to tea."

"And do you think so ill of him, father, as to believe that he would tell an untruth on the chance of getting an invitation to tea?"

"Why, no. I don't think I would go so far as to say that," said Mr. Ruberry, perceiving that he was rather on a wrong tack. "But he likes coming —there's no denying that—and if it isn't to get his tea, it must be for something else."

"What else can it be, father?"

"How should I know? You are more likely . . . I mean"—(abruptly)—"I mean that I don't want him to come any more; and if he does come, I want you not to see him."

"Why, father, what has Nelson done wrong? You were saying only the other day that he was shaping so well!" returned Miriam, with a surprised look.

"So he is. But that's nowt—I mean, it's business. Anyhow, I don't want him here."

"Because he is an apprentice, I suppose?

All the same, father, he is a gentleman—and of good breeding too."

" Who says so ? "

" It is evident in his manner and appearance."

" Well, that's the very reason I don't want him to come here," said Mr. Ruberry, with an impatient gesture, as if he found his daughter's questionings both embarrassing and irritating.

" You don't want him to come here because he is a well-bred young man! You are talking in riddles, father."

" I don't want him to come here because —because people might talk, if you will know!" blurted out Mr. Ruberry, now really angry, albeit the next moment he bitterly regretted both his display of temper and his not very discreet remark, which he would have recalled had it been possible.

" I think I understand what you mean, father, and it shall be as you wish," said Miriam, with bowed head and burning cheeks; and when tea was over she quietly withdrew.

Of all this Robert Ruberry had been keenly, though silently, observant.

" Well, if anybody had towd me, I wouldn't have believed 'em," he exclaimed, when his niece was gone.

" Believed what ? "

" That you could be such—that you could be so foolish."

" Why, what have I done ? " asked Mr. Ruberry, defiantly.

" The very thing you shouldn't have done. You've put it into her head. She'll think about nowt else now."

" Come, come now ! Didn't she say as it should be as I wished ? "

" She did say so, meaning as she wouldn't ask him here again ; but she didn't say as she wouldn't think about him."

" Well, I happen did say too much. I know I said more than I meant to do. But she put me out so with her questions. However, it's very easy to find fault : what would you have done ? "

" I would have begun at the other end—

given Nelson to understand as he isn't welcome at your house. He would have troubled
you no more after that."

"I can do so yet. But wouldn't it be best
to get rid of him altogether—send him about
his business?"

"You cannot. We are as much bound to
him as he is to us."

"We might send him back to his spinning."

"The very worst thing you could do. It
would set folks talking at once. Besides,
he is getting very useful, and the concern
would suffer. Best let it drop. At any rate,
you have put an end to her seeing him here,
and I don't suppose there is much likelihood
of her seeing him at the factory, or calling
on him at Jim Rabbits. Not as I think
there's owt between 'em, or as such a thought
has ever entered her head—unless you put
it there just now. I could tell that by her
face when she began to see what you were
driving at."

"I wish you hadn't put owt o' th' sort
into my head," growled Ben. "It has

bothered me ever since, and it bothers me yet."

"I wish I hadn't," returned Robert, with a sardonic smile. "However, as we both seem to have done our worst for our best, let's say no more about it. Some things are better let alone, and this seems to be one on 'em."

On a Sunday evening, some two or three weeks after this conversation, Robin presented himself at Oaken Cleugh and asked for an interview with its young mistress.

"Tell Miss Ruberry," he said to Phœbe, who opened the door for him, "that I have brought back her books, and should be glad to have another or two."

"Certainly, Nelson. If you'll wait here a minute I'll let her know, and bring you word," answered the maiden, graciously; for though she looked upon him as being socially rather beneath her, he had a comely face and nice manners, and the thought had more than once crossed her mind that he would make an eligible sweetheart.

In five minutes she returned.

"Miss Ruberry is sorry she cannot see you," said Phœbe; "but she will be pleased if you will step into her room and take what books you like. Shall I go with you?"

Robin, who looked very glum, nodded assent, and accompanying the maid to Miss Ruberry's room, restored to their places the books he had brought, and took two others at random.

"What a schollard you must be to read so many books, Nelson! I wish I could read," simpered Phœbe, with a killing glance of her big black eyes.

"You don't read!" said Robert, observant of the glance, but unconscious of its meaning.

"No; I wish I did. Nobody never larned me," murmured the girl, with a second glance, even more eloquent than the first.

"Why don't you go to school, then?" and with that Robin turned on his heel and left the room.

"Well, I never!" exclaimed Phœbe, in a towering passion. "Go to school, indeed! Let him go to school hissel, and larn manners.

I wouldn't have him for a sweetheart at any price—not if there wasn't another lad left at Birch Dene."

After a decent interval Robin repeated the experiment, with precisely the same result, save that Phœbe gave him a cuttingly cool reception, and he declined to take any more books.

"Tell Miss Ruberry that I am very much obliged to her, but for the present I don't require any more books," he said.

"Yes, I'll tell her," answered the young woman, with a saucy toss of her head ; " and, if I was you, I wouldn't come bothering any more about books, for I am sure she doesn't want you."

Having delivered this Parthian arrow, Phœbe, by way of driving it home, banged the door behind him, and Robin knew, as he already suspected, that he was no longer a *persona grata* at Oaken Cleugh. And he half guessed the truth—that his exclusion was more Mr. Ruberry's doing than Miriam's, for whenever they met casually, at church and

elsewhere, she always gave him the same
kindly nod, and, opportunity serving, a word
of friendly greeting. There were times, moreover, when he thought he could discern in
her beautiful eyes a wistful, pathetic look, as
if she regretted as much as he did a separation which she had been unable to avert.
But it all came to the same thing : their
pleasant meetings and fraternal relations were
at an end, and he had little hope that they
would ever be renewed.

The brothers Ruberry were naturally cog-
nizant of Robin's rebuffs. They knew that
he had been twice at Oaken Cleugh, that on
neither occasion had he been seen by Miriam,
and they gathered from Phœbe that he was
not likely to come again.

Benjamin was jubilant; he saw in this con-
summation a proof of his superior sagacity,
and crowed loudly over his would-be-wiser
brother.

"What do you say now?" he exclaimed.
"Wasn't I right in speaking to Miriam as I
did? If I hadn't, he would have been coming

yet. You're very knowing about business, I'll admit—nobody more so; but about lasses, and farming stock, and crops . . ."

"I'm not up to much, you think. Well, I never reckoned to know much about farming; it is not in my line. But about lasses I reckon to know as much as here and there an odd 'un; and I believe yet as I was quite right about Miriam," said Robert, who never, if he could help it, owned to a mistake. "I still think you went the wrong way to work. Anyhow, if I hadn't spoken, you would neither have seen nowt nor said nowt."

"Well—ay—happen," said the elder, rather taken aback by this way of putting the matter. "But I am not quite sure as there was owt to see. Folks sometimes see trees when there's no wood. However, it's happen as well as it's put a stop to. A parish apprentice, let him be as learned as he likes, is no fit companion for my lass. Have you heard as there's some talk of the Denes coming back?"

"No. When are they coming?"

"I haven't heard exactly when. To tell th' truth, I don't think as anybody knows. It's just talk. I wonder how soon after they do come back Mrs. Dene will be calling on Miriam?"

"So do I," said Robert, with one of his sarcastic laughs.

"You mean as you don't think as she will. I am sure she will. Colonel Dene is a man of his word."

"I don't deny it. But man and wife are not always of one mind, and highflyers like Mrs. Dene don't take kindly to manufacturers' daughters."

"Manufacturers' daughters! Ay, and summat more. The Ruberrys are a good old family, and I'm a country gentleman, though I am in trade."

"So you are—after a fashion. You'd be but a poor one, though, if it wasn't for th' factory. However, we shall see; and I wouldn't be so cocksure about it if I were you. It's a bad thing to be cocksure about owt."

"What an unbelieving old sinner you are, Robert! Come now; I'll bet you owt you like as Mrs. Dene comes to see Miriam."

"Ay, but when?"

"Within a month after she gets back."

"Well, I'm not much given to betting—it is not in my line—but I'll wager a five-pun note as she doesn't."

"Done with you; and I hope you'll lose, if it's only to punish you for being so doubtful about everything, and going against everything as I say. You haven't got quite all th' sense, Robert."

CHAPTER XV.

THE drawing-room at Oaken Cleugh; Miriam reclining in a rocking-chair reading a book, which, judging from the frequency with which she lays it down and thinks— or dreams—does not seem to be of absorbing interest. Are her thoughts about Robin? Possibly, for the day before she had seen him at church, and they had exchanged greetings in the porch, and when their eyes met for an instant it seemed to her that his looked reproach. And no wonder; for had she not, after promising to be his counsellor and friend, and letting him call her "sister," refused to see him when he called, and terminated their intimacy, and let nearly a twelvemonth pass without a word of explanation? Yet how could she explain—how tell him that her father . . . And as she recalled her father's words, she bowed her head and blushed as deeply as at the moment when their significance first flashed on her mind. And yet— and yet she would like to let Robin know that he had not offended her, that his exclusion from the house was not her doing, and that her sisterly affection for him was unaltered and unabated. True, she could write; but even though it were maidenly to do so (as to which she had grave doubts), it was quite out of the question, after her father's warning, to open a correspondence with Robin. For the letter would have to go either by hand or post. In the former case she would need to confide in a servant, and post letters were so few and far between that nobody at Birch Dene could get one without everybody else knowing. So there was apparently nothing for it but to wait with what patience she might for an opportunity of putting herself right with him. A word would do; she need only say that she still regarded herself as

his friend (there could surely be no harm
in that), and would always take an interest
in his welfare.

And then, trying to dismiss the subject
from her mind, she resumed her reading;
but before she had reached the bottom of
the page the door opened, and Phœbe appeared on the threshold in a state of intense
though suppressed excitement.

"The carriage from the Hall has just
turned into th' coach-road," she said, eagerly.
"It'll ten to one be Mrs. Dene. What shall
I do?"

"Show her in, of course."

"And th' footman?—it's him wi' th' big
fat coaves—must I show him in too?"

"Of course not," laughed Miriam; "he will
wait outside with the carriage."

"Thank goodness!" murmured the maid,
with a sigh of relief. "That man frightens
me; he's so grand; a peacock's a fool to
him."

Notwithstanding Miriam's seeming coolness,
she felt both nervous and excited, for Mrs.

Dene was the greatest lady in the neighbourhood, a "highflyer," as her uncle said, and
her visit a momentous event.

But her guest quickly put her at her
ease.

"At last!" she exclaimed, taking Miriam's
hand. "I promised myself this pleasure long
ago. But we were called away so suddenly,
it was quite impossible. I called on nobody.
But now we are at home for good, and I
hope we shall see much of each other. How
have you been? Very well! I am glad to
hear it. We have had, oh, such a pleasant
time in France, and my boy has grown so
much. You would hardly know him. I
would have brought him with me, but he still
feels the effect of the journey—took a little
rheum, in fact, from which he is not fully
recovered. Ah, you have been reading.
May I look? I am a great reader myself.
Molière. *Vous savez le Francais?*"—(with a
gesture of surprise).

"*Oui, madame, je le sais, un peu.*"

Whereupon Mrs. Dene said something further in the same language, but finding that Miriam knew it better than herself, she fell back on her mother tongue.

"It is so nice that you have a knowledge of French," she went on. "I have brought several French books back with me, and I shall be glad to lend them you. And we are expecting shortly a French visitor, Captain de la Faucille, an officer of the King's guard. It will be very nice for you to talk with him. He doesn't know a word of English, poor man. Yes, I enjoyed my visit to France greatly. The regiment was quartered at Boulogne, not Boulogne-sur-Mer, but Boulogne-sur-Seine, which is quite near Paris. We attended all the duke's receptions, and "assisted" at a great banquet at the Tuilleries, and went out somewhere or another nearly every evening. But I had one great anxiety. . ."

"What was that, Mrs. Dene?"

"My husband had to fight a duel. But he was very good; he did not tell me until it was over. He says it is wrong for a married man to risk his life except in his country's cause, or to save the life of another. But the quarrel was forced on him, and he had no alternative. A Bonapartist officer, a noted bully, publicly insulted Colonel Dene in a *café*, and the Colonel knocked him down. A challenge followed as a matter of course. They fought in the Bois, and . . ."

" Yes, Mrs. Dene ? "

" The Frenchman was killed."

" Oh, how dreadful ! " said Miriam with a shudder.

" It was indeed," returned Mrs. Dene, gravely ; " but it would have been much more dreadful had my husband been killed. And Captain Espinasse—that was his name—was a bloodthirsty ruffian. He made a practice of insulting and challenging our young officers, whom he invariably killed, out of revenge for Waterloo. He did not know that Colonel Dene was one of the best swordsmen in the British army. I think my husband did quite right—don't you ? He put an end to a career of murder."

" I do think so. How brave he must be ! "

exclaimed Miriam, warmly. "Birch Dene ought to be proud of him."

"I will tell him what you say; the compliment will please him," said Mrs. Dene, with a gratified smile.

She delighted to hear her husband praised.

"And, now, when will you come to see me?"

"When you please, Mrs. Dene."

"Shall we say next Thursday?"

"Certainly! If it be convenient for you, Thursday will suit me very well."

"Come early, then, in time for luncheon, and we can have a long afternoon; and Colonel Dene would like you to bring that young man with you. I forget his name, but he does something at the factory. I always call him the lost heir."

"You mean Nelson?"

"Yes; that is his name, I think."

"I don't know," said Miriam, reddening. "I mean that he has his work to do, and— I am not sure that he could be spared. He is in the counting-house now, and they find

him very useful. But if you would write
a line to my father, I dare say they would let
him come."

"Certainly if you wish it; or my husband
shall," returned Mrs. Dene, with a slight
lifting of the eyebrows, and a keen glance
at the girl. "But isn't that your father
passing the window? I might ask him now,
and save the trouble of writing."

The next moment Mr. Ruberry entered the
room, booted and spurred, a hunting-crop
under his arm and a jockey-cap in his
hand.

"I must pray you to excuse this dress,"
he said, after greeting Mrs. Dene with great
respect. "I was just starting for Toppleton,
when I heard you were here."

"Don't mention it, I beg. I always think
it is the dress which best beseems a gentleman
—especially a gentleman of the old school,
like yourself."

Mr. Ruberry (who had put on his best
company manner) smiled with all his face
and bowed in acknowledgment of the com-

pliment, which made him feel two inches higher, and at least five years younger.

"I have just been asking your daughter to take luncheon with me next Thursday."

Mr. Ruberry bowed again.

"And my husband would like Mr. Nelson to bear her company, if you would kindly let him."

"Of course, certainly—anything you like, madame," answered Mr. Ruberry, with effusion. And he would probably have said the same had she included Jim Rabbits and Old Dick in her invitation.

"On Thursday, then," said Mrs. Dene, rising from her chair and shaking hands with Miriam.

Mr. Ruberry accompanied her to her carriage, the door of which was opened by the footman with the "coaves," and as she drove off he doffed his hat and made another low bow. Miriam, looking from the window, smiled. She had no idea that her father could be so courtly. Then he returned to the drawing-room, exultant.

"Didn't I tell you so?" he exclaimed, with a boisterous laugh, clapping Miriam on the shoulder. "I knew as she'd come. And wasn't I right when I said you would get asked to th' Hall—though you are but a tradesman's daughter. I wonder what your Uncle Robert will say now? Anyhow, I'll make him pay me that five pounds, and thou shall have it, lass, to spend as thou likes."

Robert did not say very much, but he contrived to take the gilt off his brother's gingerbread for all that.

"You're right for once," he said; "and Mrs. Dene has more common sense and neighbourly feeling than I gave her credit for; but I don't see what occasion there is for so much fratching (boasting). Nelson has to go, too, hasn't he? That looks as if she doesn't see so much difference between a parish apprentice and—what shall we say?—a country gentleman's daughter. Does it? And, what's more, they'll be thrown together again. However, if it suits you, I have nowt to say against it."

This was a consequence which, in his excitement, Mr. Ruberry had overlooked. He had almost forgotten, in fact, that he had promised to let the young fellow bear his daughter company.

"What a kill-joy you are, Robert!" he exclaimed, in a deeply mortified tone. "I never make the least bit of a mistake that you don't pounce on it at once. But I don't think Mrs. Dene had the least idea of putting Nelson on th' same level as Miriam. It's just a whim of the Colonel's. And I willn't let him go with her—I'll be hanged if I will. It came so sudden, I really hadn't time to think."

"Nay, nay; that would never do. You must keep your promise, or else the fat will be in the fire with a vengeance. If one goes, t'other must go. It's a pity you hadn't presence of mind to make an excuse; you could easily have said as he couldn't be spared, or as you would speak to me. However, it cannot be helped now. You'll just have to make th' best of it."

"Ay, it is a pity," repeated Benjamin,

ruefully : " but to tell th' honest truth, I was that pleased when I saw Mrs. Dene I never gave Nelson a thought, confound him ! But it's not likely to happen again ; and I don't suppose any harm will come of it. Miriam's a sensible lass."

" Well, there's no telling. Harm does oft come of it when lasses and lads gets together. However, we'll hope for th' best," said Robert, with an exasperating smile—so exasperating that his brother disdained to reply.

The next question that arose was how Miriam should travel. Birch Dene Hall was within easy walking distance of Oaken Cleugh, but Mr. Ruberry did not deem it becoming for his daughter to proceed thither on foot. To send her in the gig, he thought, would be equally *infra dig.*, and as the old chaise, when overhauled, was found to be in an extremely dilapidated condition (it had not been used since the late Mrs. Ruberry's death), there was nothing for it but to get one from Manchester, and horse it with a pair of Mr. Ruberry's own animals. Still, another difficulty was the disposal of Robin. To let him walk while Miriam rode might, feared Mr. Ruberry, give offence at the Hall. On the other hand, to let him go inside the chaise with Miriam was quite out of the question for several reasons. So the matter was compromised by putting him on the box with our old friend Gib Riding, who, in default of the ostler (laid up with rheumatism), had to act as coachman.

Mr. Ruberry flattered himself that he managed this rather delicate business with consummate address, so contriving matters as to keep the young people apart without letting his object be perceived.

After informing Robin of the invitation, and telling him to be sure to " behave " (as if he had been a small boy), he observed, loftily, and as if it were quite an afterthought—

" If you'll be up at our house about half-past twelve, you may happen ride in th' chaise."

Robin, it need hardly be said, was punctual to the minute, and he had an opportunity of greeting Miriam as she stepped into the chaise.

"I think you'd better get on the box, and see as Gib doesn't take th' stoop [drive against a post]," he said, half laughing, to Robin. Then, in an undertone, "See as he drives careful, specially coming back. Gib isn't as good a whip as Carroty Joe [the ostler]. Captain hasn't been in double harness afore, and I shouldn't like there to be any lumber. I'm a bit doubtful how he'll shap."

Robin, after promising faithful compliance with these instructions, took his place beside Gib, and the team went at a slapping pace down the avenue—for, though Mr. Ruberry sometimes kept a screw, he had a rooted objection to a slug.

"It's a different consarn this fro' that owd cart as I once druv yo' fro' Manchester in, isn't it?" said Gib, proudly, as they turned into the main road. "Th' mayster thinks as I corn't tool a pair o' hosses. He wor never more mista'en in his life. I worn't three year in a coaching stable for nowt. I'll drive wi' onybody, whether it be a ploo or a post-chaise. Bithmon, I never thowt as I should be driving yo' to th' Ho wi' th' young missus! Yo' 've getting on, yo' have that. And yo' desarve to get on, if it's nobbut for never axing me for that shilling as yo' lant me when yo' coom at fost—and that's going i' two years sin'. I'd ha' paid yo', but I haven't had as mich i' my pocket sin'—I haven't, as true as . . . Th' wife olus draws my wage, and hoo willn't gi' me more than sixpence a week for beer brass. . . Whoa! Steady, Captain!—and it's hard slacking yer thirst on sixpence a week. However, I reckon as yo' and me's more than straight now, and yo'll be in my debt to th' tune of eighteenpence after to-day."

"I in your debt to the tune of eighteenpence! How on earth do you make that out? Why, you owe me a shilling. But as it's so long since . . ."

"Come now! Don't yo' think as driving yo' and th' young missus to th' Ho in a chaise and pair desarves hoaf a crown—and th' chaise

new done up and th' hosses as fresh as paint.
Eighteenpence 'll just sattle it. . . . And
I olus said as yo' wor a gentleman i' th'
bottom; and your fayther wor one afore
yo', I'll be bun!"

Robin laughed, but the appeal, backed by
so handsome a compliment, was irresistible.
Gib got his eighteenpence.

" I knew yo' would," he said, complacently
pocketing the money; "and if ever I hear
onybody say as yore not a gradely gentleman,
I'll punch his shins for him. . . And
look yo' here, now! If yo' like to get inside
as we come back I'll say nowt—a nod's as
good as a wink, you know. It'll be to'ard
th' edge o' dark, I darsay, and I'm sure
hoo'd liefer have yore company than be
boxed up aw by hersel'; and yore not th' lad
I take yo' for if yo'd have owt ageean it.
Whoa, Captain! Did thou never see a black
jackass afore, thou goamless beggar?"

CHAPTER XVI.

AT DENE HALL.

An old historic mansion was Birch Dene Hall, the oldest part of it dating from the time of the first Tudor, to which had been added one wing in the Elizabethan style, and another in that of Queen Anne, the whole forming a somewhat incongruous yet picturesque building—a quaint mixture of dormer-windows, timbered walls, high gables, and red chimney-stacks, clothed in a mantle of creeping ivy. Before the terraced front stretched the park—a wide expanse of undulating turf, studded with grand old trees—and the long avenue wound between a double row of ancient elms, which in summer met overhead and made a cool and grateful shade.

"If I lived here I couldn't help being as happy as a king, even if I'd to wait on mysel' and nowt to eat but porridge and blue milk; and they say as Colonel Dene has ten thousand a year, to say nowt of his handsome wife and that bonnie little lad," observed Gib, as they sighted the house.

The same thought occurred to Robin. It was impossible not to envy the owner of such a fine old place and so beautiful a domain.

As they drove up to the door the gentleman in question, with a gun under his arm and a brace of setters at his heel, rounded the corner of the house. On seeing the carriage he hurried forward, and was just in time to help Miriam to alight. Colonel Dene greeted his guests cordially, and with less of formality than was customary at the period. Then he took them round the building, pointing out some of its more remarkable characteristics, and relating a little of its history. The outer door, of massive oak, was studded with enormous nails, and pitted here and there with bullet-holes, the bullets being still quite visible.

"We are supposed to be very proud of these bullet-marks," said Colonel Dene, pleasantly. "My wife thinks all the world of them, and they certainly are an interesting historical relic—although, if I had been living at the time, I fancy I should have been among those who made them."

"You mean that the house was held for the king, and the bullets were fired by the Roundheads?" asked Robin.

"Exactly; and a brave defence the garrison made of it—I will say that for them, albeit I think they were on the wrong side. But come in, and I will show you something of which I am proud."

As the Colonel spoke he led the way into a spacious hall, panelled in oak, whereon hung trophies of arms, tattered and moth-eaten banners, and old family portraits, which looked down on several suits of ancient armour, standing erect on their pedestals.

"What a glorious old place!" exclaimed Robin, enthusiastically. "It is like seeing history, or the realization of a dream. How proud of it you must be, Colonel Dene!"

"All the more so as I wasn't brought up in the expectation that it could by any possibility ever be mine. Yes, it is a dear old place. See! Here is something of which I am a good deal prouder than of the bullet-marks I showed you just now. This harness was worn by an ancestor of mine at Flodden Field. He led a hundred archers of Birch to the battle, and, according to tradition, their cloth-yard shafts did dire execution among the Scots on that famous day. There is a fine description of the battle in *Marmion*. Perhaps you may have heard of it—by Scott, you know, who wrote *The Lay of the Last Minstrel.*"

"Oh, yes," said Robin. "I know *Marmion ;*" and, with great fire and animation, he repeated the well-known lines, descriptive of Flodden fight.

"Who is this declaiming Scott?" said

Mrs. Dene, who had entered the hall unperceived, as Robin, remembering where he was,
paused in some confusion. " I was not aware
you were a reader of poetry, and could recite
it so well, Mr. Nelson."

" He has read a good deal, I think," observed
Colonel Dene, regarding him thoughtfully.
" Would you like to look round the library
until luncheon is ready, Nelson ? "

Robin answered in the affirmative, and as
Mrs. Dene led Miriam off in one direction,
the Colonel led him off in another.

The library was a spacious room, furnished
in oak, and with deeply embayed windows,
between which hung a few choice paintings,
while the inner walls were covered with
books from floor to ceiling, and from end
to end.

" We have a vast number of old works,
as you see," remarked the Colonel. " Nobody
reads them now. But I think we have also
the best of modern and contemporary authors.
Here are Scott's poems, for instance, Have
you read any of his novels ? There is a new

one just out, *The Bride of Lammermoor*—to my thinking, one of the finest tragedies in the language."

"No, sir, I have never had the opportunity. I cannot afford to buy books. *Marmion* was lent to me."

"Would you like to take one of these with you? They are splendid stories, and I am sure would entertain you. We have them all. The Waverley novels too . . ."

"How are you getting on with the Ruberrys?" asked Colonel Dene, after Robin had accepted the offer and tendered his thanks. "It must be horrible, living in that apprentice house. At least, I have heard so."

"I don't live there now, sir. I have been promoted."

"To what?"

Robin told him.

"I am very glad. Yet, still—Miss Ruberry seems to be a very nice young woman. Is she as good as she looks?"

"As good as she looks! Yes—quite,"

stammered Robin, surprised, as well he might be, by the suddenness and irrelevancy of the question. "Quite as good—and better."

"Better than she looks! She must be very good, then. I suppose people like her?"

"Yes, sir. Everybody likes Miss Ruberry. She has persuaded her uncle to establish an infirmary in connection with the apprentice house. She looks after it herself, and goes a good deal among the tenants. It is thought she would do much more if Mr. Robert would let her. But, as it is, she has made great changes, and since she came home, the place is altogether brighter and better."

"Well, from all I have heard, great changes were required at Factory Hollow, as folks call it. How is that poor devil we locked up going on?"

"Blincoe! He has grown a good deal, and begins to look something like a man. I don't think, though, that his imprisonment did him much good."

"How so?"

"It seems to have made him more sullen and revengeful, and he sometimes says things which makes me fear that, occasion serving, he may try to revenge himself. They say he set Lowdham Mills on fire— the place he was at before he came to Birch Dene."

"I hope he won't do anything of that sort here; he is not likely to get off with imprisonment if he does. Fire-raising is a capital offence, and he would not get much mercy. Why should he hanker so after revenge. Has he been ill-used?"

"Terribly. Worse than a negro slave."

"Well, these factory masters, like everybody else, must reap as they have sown. . . . You are young, Nelson. Let me impress on you this lesson: As you sow now, so will you reap. No man can do wrong—ay, or shrink from doing right—without paying the penalty. Even an honest error of judgment may cause widespread misery. . . Have you warned your employers of Blincoe's threats?"

"They hardly amount to threats. And

it would be of no use speaking to Mr.
Robert. He despises the hands too much
to fear them. And he has been threatened
so often, without anything coming of it, that
he would give no heed—perhaps not even
hear me. Besides, I don't like to report ex-
pressions that I have accidentally overheard.
The only effect would be to get Blincoe
punished, and so make him more revengeful
than ever."

"Well, perhaps you are right. But couldn't
you speak to Mr. Ruberry?"

"Mr. Ruberry leaves the management
nearly altogether to his brother. He would
simply refer me to him, and I should probably
be set down as a busybody. And Blincoe
has really said very little that can be laid
hold of. I judge more from his character
and his antecedents than his words. I may
be quite wrong."

"Let us hope you are. You were speaking
of Mr. Ruberry. Do you know anything of
his late wife—who she was, or where she came
from?"

"Nothing whatever, sir. I dare say Miss Ruberry could tell you."

"I dare say she could"—(dryly). "Have you heard anything more of the gentleman you were telling me about—I forget his name—who persuaded you to become an apprentice?"

"Moses Weevil. No; but I should very much like to have a word with him. What lies he and that beadle did tell me!"

"He must have wanted to get rid of you very badly."

"I begin to think so. All the same, I cannot tell why. Solomon thought Mr. Bartlett had made a will in my favour, and that Weevil had destroyed it. But in that case why should he want to get me out of the way? I had no claim either on him or on the estate."

"Mr. Bartlett wasn't akin to you, then?"

"Not the least; though if I had been really his son, he could not have treated me more kindly. He did more for me than my father. Not that I blame my father; it is no fault of his."

"How then? . . . But there goes the luncheon-bell. We must continue our talk afterwards. I should like to know more of Mr. Bartlett and yourself—if I may."

After the apprentice house and Jim Rabbits's cottage, it was a strange experience for Robin to find himself sitting next to Miriam in that grand old dining-room, as assiduously waited on by a butler so intensely solemn and respectable that he could hardly help calling him "Sir," and a tall footman with powdered hair, as if he had been a young lord instead of a nameless waif. Miriam was as bright and cheerful as usual, and she and Mrs. Dean did the principal part of the talking. The host, though he said little, was quietly observant. Robin said even less, and seemed more thoughtful than befitted the occasion—perhaps because his recent conversation with Colonel Dean had roused painful memories.

When luncheon was over, the Colonel suggested a walk round the grounds and a visit to the stables—a proposal in which Miriam and Robin gladly concurred ; and Mrs. Dene, who lost no opportunity of exhibiting her son and heir, sent for the boy that he might accompany them.

The gardens were as old-fashioned as the house—straight walks, rectangular grass-plots, shrubs cut into the shapes of birds and beasts, with here and there a mossy fountain and a fish-pond full of fat carp. The conservatories and vine-houses greatly delighted Miriam, and an agreeable hour was spent in inspecting the horticultural treasures they contained.

"Now for the stables," said Colonel Dene; and he was leading the way thither when a servant came to inform him that Mr. Alport, from Manchester, had just arrived, and desired to see him on business.

"If it is business, you had better go at once, Eustace," observed Mrs. Dene. "I can show our guests round the stables, and we will follow you presently."

"Yes, perhaps it were better so. I do not like to keep people waiting, and if Mr. Alport has not gone when you return, Nelson would perhaps like to go into the library and look at the books until I can join him."

The stables were in excellent order, and the horses well-bred and in high condition. Robin admired them as much as Miriam had admired the conservatories; and "Master Dene," as his mother, when speaking to "inferiors," always called her son, insisted on being placed astride his pony, which was little bigger than a Newfoundland mastiff.

"He is young to begin riding, but I want him to be a consummate horseman. Every gentleman should ride well"—(strong emphasis on "gentleman"). "Do you ride, Mr. Nelson?" asked Mrs. Dene.

⹁ "I have a faint recollection of riding either a pony or a donkey when I was a small boy, and when factory masters begin to provide their apprentices with saddle-horses, I shall probably have a chance of riding again," laughed Robin.

"That is not very likely, I fear; but I thought, perhaps . . . Would you mind helping Master Dene to dismount from his pony,

Mr. Nelson? Thank you. Now I think we
have seen pretty nearly everything, and if
you have no objection, we will retrace our
steps. Are you tired, Miss Ruberry?"

"Not in the least. I never tire of walking
in a garden—your grounds are so very beautiful; and I could look at the house for ever.
I have enjoyed my visit vastly, thanks to your
kindness, Mrs. Dene. Haven't you, Nelson?"

"I don't think I ever enjoyed anything
so much. Master Dene is very fortunate in
being heir to so fine a property."

"You are quite right, he is"—(looking
fondly at the boy). "All the same, I hope
it will be a long time before he comes into
possession. My dear husband is still in the
prime of life. Yet we cannot live for ever,
and it is pleasant to think that the property is
not likely to pass into the hands of strangers
—that the son will succeed the father. . . .
Here we are at the Hall. There is the library,
Mr. Nelson. I have no doubt Colonel Dene
will soon have done with Mr. Alport. This
way, if you please, Miss Ruberry."

After making the tour of the library, and examining with professional interest some of the older books, he sought the copy of *The Bride of Lammermoor*, of which Colonel Dene had spoken, and seating himself in a big arm-chair, began to read the first volume of that incomparable novel. But hardly had he opened the book when he gave a sort of gasp, looked up with an expression of intense bewilderment, and then, springing from his chair, walked hurriedly round the room.

"At last, at last!" he murmured. "I have found my name—I have found my name! Never, please Heaven, to forget it more! It is almost the same as that in the book. How strange! I will look again."

And with that he sat down a second time, and, still holding the volume in his hand, became so absorbed in thought that he heard neither the opening of the door nor the footsteps of his hosts.

"You seem interested, Nelson. Deep in a

book—eh? What is it?" asked Colonel Dene.

"*The Bride of Lammermoor*, sir," said Robin, with a start of surprise.

"I knew you would like it. It is a splendid dramatic story, but the *dénouement* is tragical. I confess I don't much like tragedies, though if novels be true to life, they cannot always end happily. And it is well to show how cruel a strong-willed, over-bearing woman can be, even to her own child. Is your mother still alive, Nelson?"

"No, sir. My mother died long ago."

"And your father?"

"I only just remember him, sir," answered Robin, evasively; for he felt that if he continued to answer the Colonel's questions he would end in telling him all, and he shrank from letting this gentleman, who was so kind to him, know that he was the son of a woman who had been convicted of a capital felony.

"You are very unfortunate to be cast on the world at so early an age without a parent's care. I have always a deep sympathy for young men situated as you are. I never saw my own mother after I was thirteen. How old are you?"

"Exactly the same age as the century."

"So you were born in 1800—twenty years ago?"

"Yes, sir."

And then the Colonel, either perceiving that the young fellow answered his questions reluctantly, or not liking to be inquisitive, took up a newspaper and left him to read in peace—or rather to think, as, albeit his eyes were on the book, his thoughts were far away.

After a while there came a knock at the door, and a servant, quietly entering, informed his master that coffee was served in the morning room.

"Come, let us join the ladies," said the Colonel, rising from his chair. "Drinking a cup of coffee in the afternoon is a habit I contracted in the West Indies, where it was once my ill-fortune to spend several years."

"Who is Mr. Alport, Eustace, and what does he want?" asked Mrs. Dene, as she handed her husband a cup of coffee.

"He is the chief constable's secretary, or something of the sort, and he wants the local justices to suppress or proclaim—I don't know what is the correct legal term—a reform meeting which the Radicals are proposing to hold shortly in this neighbourhood."

"And what answer did you give him?"

"None. I told him that I should like to make further inquiries before consenting to any such proceeding. Order must be maintained, of course; but I do not gather that any breach of the peace is apprehended. Alport says there will be seditious speeches, and urges that prevention is better than cure."

"And don't you think it is?"

"As a general principle, certainly. But I have only Alport's word for it that the speeches would be seditious; and who is to define sedition? It were better, in my opinion, to let the meeting take place, and

then, if any of the speakers do spout sedition,
prosecute them. For my part, I confess that
I rather sympathize with these reformers.
The country is in a very unsatisfactory condition, and the Government seems to have no
remedy but repression—if it be a remedy. A
soldier on active service has no business to
take a prominent part in politics, even if he
could, and I have been campaigning the
greater part of my life ; but now that I have
a free hand . . ."

" You would surely not openly take sides
with these Radicals, Eustace !" interposed
Mrs. Dene, with an alarmed look.

" I am not at all sure that I shall not. At
any rate, I will have no hand in suppressing
their meetings—so long as they keep the
peace. Do you know a man of the name of
Romford, Nelson ? "

" Yes, sir ; he is a silk weaver. It was he
who lent me *Marmion.*"

" He has literary tastes, then ? "

" Yes ; he writes poetry, and is extremely
well read."

"And speaks at Radical meetings?"

"I believe so; but I think he is a man of very moderate views, and he takes even greater interest in books than in politics."

"I am afraid, though, that won't prevent him from getting into trouble. His very moderation makes against him. The police think it is put on as a blind, and suspect him of holding secret relations with the physical force people; and Alport more than hinted that if Mr. Romford does not mind what he is about, he is very likely to be arrested. As you know the man, it might be a kindness to put him on his guard."

Robin was about to say that he certainly would put Romford on his guard, when a footman appeared and announced that Miss Ruberry's carriage was at the door, and as both Miriam and himself feared to outstay their welcome, they hastened to take their leave. Before they went away, Mrs. Dene expressed the hope that she would soon have the pleasure of seeing Miriam again; and the Colonel, after reminding Robin not to forget

The Bride of Lammermoor, told him to come to the Hall whenever he liked, and borrow from the library any book he might fancy.

"Nothing is more unfair," he said, "than to monopolize books. They are so costly that only the well-to-do can afford to buy them, and it is the duty of those who have, to lend to those who have not."

And so this memorable visit came to an end, but not quite in the way which Mr. Ruberry had planned; for Robin, contrary to his master's expectations and oblivious of his injunctions, followed Miriam into the chaise and took the seat opposite to hers.

"You here?" she exclaimed, with a look of surprise.

"I beg your pardon—I had no idea—I mean I did not intend—I wasn't thinking. Shall I get out and go on the box?" he said with bated breath.

"Of course you must get out—and at once. But, no, not now. We are off, and it would look so strange to stop the carriage in the

avenue.   Wait till we have passed the lodge
gates."

"Yes.   I will wait till we have passed the
lodge gates," said Robin, humbly.   "Miriam
—I beg your pardon—I mean Miss Ruberry."

"You may call me Miriam—when nobody
is by.   I am still your sister."

"You are!"—(joyfully).   "Then why do
you always refuse to see me and keep out of
my way?"

"I cannot tell you.   It is not my wish; it
is my duty.   I cannot see you at Oaken
Cleugh any more."

"But do tell me why, Miriam.   Otherwise
I shall think the fault lies with me—that I
have offended you, or you have heard something to my detriment."

"Not at all.   Did I not say that I am still
your sister? And now don't ask me any more
questions.   If you do I shall not answer."

"So!   I was right, then, in thinking I
wasn't wanted at Oaken Cleugh."

"That is asking—I never said so—but
perhaps.   You forget, I think, that though

Oaken Cleugh is my home it is not my house.
Let that suffice "—(peremptorily).

After this a spell of silence, which Robin
was the first to break.

"Miriam!" he said, softly, as they passed
the lodge gates.

"If you ask any more . . ."

"I am not going to ask. I'm going to tell
you something—something that will surprise
you . . ."

"Yes, Robin. What is it?"—(eagerly).

"I know my name."

"You know your name! How?"

"I found one so like it in this book—*The
Bride of Lammermoor*—that the very moment
I set eyes on it I remembered my own."

"And that is . . . ?"

"Ravensmere. My name is Ravensmere,
Miriam."

"Ravensmere! Why, that was Colonel
Dene's name before he came into the property.
It is one of his names still."

"But—but—it seems impossible. How do
you know? Who told you?" exclaimed

Robin, excitedly. "Oh, no, I cannot believe it."

"Mrs. Dene told me. We were talking about the old Denes, and she said her husband, though descended from them on his mother's side, was really a Ravensmere. His full name is William Eustace Ravensmere Dene. . . Oh, Robin!—the carriage! It is turning over! We shall be killed! Help! Oh!"

A violent swaying of the chaise—an exclamation of dismay from Gib—a rattle of iron hoofs on the splash-board—and a shriek from Miriam as she is thrown against Robin, who, by way of shielding her from harm, folds her in a tight embrace.

CHAPTER XVII.

A SENSIBLE LASS.

IT was not a very big smash, and no great harm was done. Robin received on his hat and partly on his head a piece of broken glass, which, but for his promptitude in protecting Miriam as he did, might have cut her face and hurt her seriously. With some difficulty he opened the door, and, after scrambling out, extricated his companion—as the carriage was still wobbling about, a somewhat delicate operation.

"Oh, Robin, I am so thankful you were with me!" exclaimed Miriam, fervently. "Whatever should I have done?"

Two wheels of the chaise were in the ditch —two in the air. Gib, with nose badly barked, and clothes covered with mud, was at the horses' heads trying to pacify Captain, who plunged violently, and showed a strong disposition to kick himself loose.

"Why, Gib, you are drunk!" said Robin, regarding him closely.

"Well, I wor a bit on a while sin', that's true; but this do has gradely sobered me. It's aw along o' that eighteenpence as yo' gan me; I supped it welly aw at th' 'Hare and Hounds.' But it wornt my fault—not a bit. I couldn't ha' driven moor careful if th' chaise had been a hearse and yo' two corpses wi' brass plates on th' lids. It wor that black jackass, th' same as Captain shied at as we wor coming. And it had milk-kits on its back this time, and th' Owd Lad doesn't hate holy water moor than Captain hates a black jackass wi' them fangling things on its back. He connot abide 'em."

"Never mind the black jackass," said Robin, sharply. "What is to be done? That is the question."

"Will yo' unyoke th' hosses while I howd 'em? There's no use trying to poo th' chaise out ; th' tackle isn't strong enough. . . Whoa, Captain ! Steady, Smiler, my lad ! That's it. We mun have some strength and a plank or two to get them hind wheels out o' th' dyke bottom. Th' best thing as yo' and th' young missus can do is to go home by th' pad gate (footpath) as fast as yo' can, and send some o' th' chaps here, while I bide wi' th' hosses."

"Come, Miriam, let us go at once," said Robin. "We can do it in twenty minutes by the fields."

"Don't forget to tell th' mayster as th' hosses is no waur, and it wor aw along o' that theer black jackass, curse it ! " shouted Gib, as they set off.

" I am afraid my father will be very angry," said Miriam.

" That is very likely, I think. He told me to stop on the box with Gib, and see that he drove carefully coming back, and instead of that I got inside with you. But really I was so full of what I had just learnt, and wanted so much to tell you. . . "

"It was very well you did come inside. If you hadn't, I am sure I should have been badly hurt. The glass that fell on your hat would have fallen on my face, and perhaps blinded me. Oh, Robin, your head is cut! It is bleeding terribly. Let me tie this handkerchief round it."

"I don't think it is very much—only skin deep," said Robin, carelessly; but he made no objection to the handkerchief.

"What shall we say to my father?" asked Miriam, when the operation, which perhaps took more time than was absolutely necessary, came to an end.

"I'll take the blame, say that it was all my fault—that I quite forgot myself, in fact; and when you wanted me to get out I refused."

"Oh, Robin, that wouldn't be true! It was just the other way about. You wanted to get out, and I wouldn't let you. Besides, I won't let you take all the blame. I shall say that I wanted you to stay inside with me for company till we passed the lodge gates, and that if you had not done so I should have been very badly hurt ; that it was really quite providential—and it was."

"Do you think that is an explanation which will satisfy your father ? "

"I do. He will be so delighted that I am safe, that he will never think of finding fault with you."

"And if he does, I don't think I shall care much now that I know my own name my father's."

"Your father's ! "

"Yes. For if my name is Ravensmere, so must be my father's."

"And Ravensmere was Colonel Dene's name. Do you think—can it be possible ? "

"The same thought has occurred to you, then ? Yes, Miriam, I believe that Colonel Dene is my father."

"Then you would be . . . Oh, Robin, I cannot realize it ! He is the lord of the manor. It seems impossible. Are you sure ? "

"It isn't possible to be sure—yet. But I believe so ; although there are several things that I cannot understand. His name was William Ravensmere—so was my father's. Whether he was also called ' Eustace ' I don't know ; he may have been. My father was a soldier—so is Colonel Dene ; and they must be about the same age. The Colonel mentioned to-day that he was a long time in the West Indies. My father was also a long time in the West Indies."

" There cannot be a doubt of it, Robin ; it must be so."

" Wait a moment. I said there were some things I did not understand. My father was in the Marines—the Colonel belongs to a line regiment ; and I did not gather, from what your father said the last time I was at your house, that he was ever married before —that when he married the present Mrs. Dene he was a widower. Did you ever hear anything of the sort ? "

" No ; and I scarcely could have done, seeing how much I have been from home."

" That is true. All the same I should like to find out. If he has been twice married,

my belief would become certainty. But
then . . ."

Here the young fellow hesitated, and his
countenance became troubled.

" You were saying, Robin . . ."

" A very unpleasant thought crossed my
mind, Miriam. How could my father marry
a second time while ignorant of my mother's
fate ? For anything he knew she might still
be living, and if any inquiry had been made, I
should surely have heard. No, it must be
some other Ravensmere—perhaps a cousin
of the Colonel's."

" Why not tell him your story, and ask
him the question ? "

" Because . . . I have thought over and
over again how I should act when I found
my father. How I should act, what I should
say, and what he would say. I used to think
that it would be very straightforward and
simple—that he would recognize me as easily
as I should recognize him. But lately I have
thought differently—perhaps because I have
gained in experience, and seen more of the

world and its ways. And, as you see, the
Colonel and I have not recognized each other.
Then, again, how am I to prove my statement?
Wouldn't it look very strange if, the day
after hearing that his name used to be Ravensmere, I should go to him and say, 'My name
is also Ravensmere, and I am your son.' Anybody could say his name was Ravensmere;
and I have read stories about false claimants.
I read one not long ago."

"But surely the Colonel would be glad
to find his long-lost son, and he could make
inquiry as to the truth of your statements."

"Is it so sure that he would be glad to find
his long-lost son?" said Robin, sadly. "I
have always thought that my father would
be as glad to find me as I should be to find
him; and when the thought has occasionally
occurred to me that he had possibly no wish
to hear anything more either of his wife or
his son, I have said to myself, 'It is impossible. My father is an officer and a gentleman.' But if Colonel Dene be my father, he
must have married a second wife without

making sure that the first was dead; and I am afraid he would not be very pleased to know that I am alive."

"But perhaps he did make sure."

"He could not well have made sure without hearing that his son was alive, which would be a worse sign still."

"So it would. What will you do, then, Robin?"

"Well, the first thing is to find out whether the Colonel has been married before."

"That is easily managed. I can ask my father in such a way that he will not guess my motive; and if he does not know, I will ask Mrs. Sirricold. She is a great gossip, and knows everything about everybody."

"The Rector's wife?"

"Yes; but it seems to me that you should ask the advice of some experienced person."

"I should be very glad; but who is there? Your father and uncle . . ."

"They wouldn't do at all. I think my father would believe you—at any rate, until he had a talk with my uncle. But he couldn't keep your secret an hour, and my uncle . . ."

"Wouldn't believe a word I said. And as for Jim Rabbits . . . Stay, I have it! Romford is the man."

"What! The Radical weaver, whom my uncle so much detests!"

"The same. But your uncle's detestation is no proof that the weaver is not a good fellow. Romford comes occasionally to Rabbits on the quiet, so as not to get Jim into trouble with your uncle. He is very shrewd, and I think I might safely trust him."

"But wouldn't you do better to consult some man of education, or a lawyer?"

"Romford is a man of education—though for the most part he has educated himself, I fancy. He is very well read, spends all his spare money in books, and has seen a good deal of the world—been at sea, and tramped all over England. A lawyer might be better. But how could I consult a lawyer? There are only two at Toppleton—one of whom acts for the firm, the other for Colonel Dene."

" It must be Romford, then. When will you see him ? "

" As soon as possible. When will you let me know the result of your inquiry ? "

Also as soon as possible. But how shall I communicate with you ? Let me see. . . . I have to be at the hospital about eleven on Saturday morning. Could you contrive to be there at the same time ? "

" Easily. But . . ."

" I know what you are going to say. We shall not be alone. But listen. I shall bring a book with me, and I shall say quite loud : ' Here, Nelson, is a very nice book, which you might read to the apprentices.' Then, when you are by yourself, you will open the book, and between the leaves you will find a note."

" Capital ! " exclaimed Robin, gleefully. " What a splendid idea ! And when I return the book I will put into it another note, telling you what Romford advises, and how I am going on."

" I shall be very glad. But you must not

give the book to Phœbe. The note might drop out."

" No it won't. I'll put the note between two of the leaves, and then gum the edges together."

" Still, it would be as well . . ."

" Of course I shall give the book into your hands if I can see you, and failing that, put it into the book-case myself; and if you would tell me beforehand in what other book you would put your answer, I could borrow it—don't you see ? "

" If an answer should be needful. Well, I'll think about it, and let you know when I write. . . . No, I don't think it would be wrong. My father did not forbid me to write to you, and if it turns out that you are a Ravensmere, I dare say he will for- give me "—(smiling). . . . " Oh, Robin, I never thought of that before. If you are the Colonel's son, you will be the heir, won't you ? "

" I never thought of it before, either. Shall I ? " said Robin, dubiously.

" Of course you will. The eldest is always the heir, and you are the eldest. And I

know somebody who won't like it — Mrs.
Dene. She is so much set up in her boy,
and so proud of his being the heir."

"Poor little fellow! I should be sorry to
put his nose out of joint."

"But you cannot help it; it is not your
fault that you are the first-born."

"You are counting my chickens before
they are hatched. Suppose my father refuses
to acknowledge me?"

"Oh, but he must. . . . Isn't that Binfield
farmhouse? How slowly we must have
walked! I had no idea. Let us hurry on,
or it will be dark before we get home."

Meanwhile Mr. Ruberry was awaiting the
return of his daughter in a condition of
pleasurable expectancy. He liked the idea
of her driving home from her visit to the
Hall in a State carriage, and was exceedingly
curious to know "how she had gone on."
During the day he could hardly talk about
anything else, until Robert shut him up by
disrespectfully comparing him to a clucking
hen that had just laid a big egg, and ex-

pressing a hope that his egg would not "turn out to be addled."

When Mr. Ruberry went home (much earlier than usual), he inquired pompously whether his daughter had returned from the Hall (though he knew very well she had not), and about the time of her expected arrival he went into the garden, and paced about where he might enjoy the sight of the carriage coming up the avenue, Miriam inside, Robin and Gib on the box.

"It would never have done to let that lad ride inside," he said to himself—"never have done at all. It wouldn't have looked respectable; and though Miriam's a sensible lass, and I don't think there's owt in what Robert says—he's always so suspicious—and she behaved so well when I spoke to her about Nelson coming up to th' house, there's no telling, and it's always best to be on th' safe side. 'A stitch in time saves nine,' as my mother used to say. And with her inside and him outside, they are as wide asunder as if they weren't in th' same parish; and they wouldn't be thrown together much at th' Hall—there's too many of 'em for that . . . Hello! Who can them two be coming up th' road? . . . It looks like . . . Bithmon, it is—Miriam and Nelson, and him with a clout round his head! What the devil is up now, I wonder?"

And with that Mr. Ruberry hurried down the avenue to meet the returning wanderers.

"What's to do now?" he exclaimed. "Why are you walking? What's become of Gib and th' carriage? I sent him off to fetch you back nearly two hours since."

"We left the carriage in a ditch, close to the milestone this side of Dene Hall lodge gates," said Miriam, calmly, as if leaving your carriage in a ditch bottom was the most ordinary of occurrences. And Robin thought that in thus acting she showed great tact. It was far better than getting excited and making a fuss.

"Why—how—what the devil did you do that for?" asked Mr. Ruberry, not at all calmly, and growing very red in the face.

" We have had an accident, father ; nothing serious—though Nelson has got his head rather badly cut. The horses are none the worse, and I don't think the carriage has taken much harm. I will tell you all about it"—which she did both cleverly and ingenuously ; for though she kept nothing back, she made everything appear to the best, and concluded with mentioning Gib's requisition for planks and "strength."

Nevertheless, Mr. Ruberry, albeit somewhat appeased, seemed far from satisfied.

" Didn't I tell you to stop on the box and see as Gib drove careful ? " he asked Robin, sternly.

" You did, sir ; but when the footman at the Hall held the chaise-door open after Mi—ss Ruberry got in—evidently expecting me to follow—I did so, quite forgetful of your injunction. I am very sorry ; but I was only inside a very short time . . .".

" And he was going to get out after we passed the lodge gates," added Miriam. " He would have got out before, but I thought Mr. and Mrs. Dene would think it looked strange; and it was very well he did not. If I had been by myself my face would have been cut all to pieces. You should thank Nelson instead of blaming him, father."

"Thank him! What will you say next, I wonder?" exclaimed Mr. Ruberry, looking very much surprised. "If he had done as I told him, and looked after Gib, there would have been no lumber [catastrophe]. It's all his fault, that's what it is. It's nowt else."

"How can you say so, father? Didn't I tell you that Captain shied at a black donkey with two milk-tins on its back? How could Nelson have prevented that, wherever he had been? Could you have prevented it, father?"

"Well, happen not," returned Mr. Ruberry, rather weakly succumbing to this *argumentum ad hominem*. "If it had been owt else it would have been different. But Captain never could stand a black jackass——"

"And this was a very black one, father. Gib says it was the blackest he ever saw."

"And the horses are no worse?"

"Not a bit! There's nobody hurt but

Nelson. But don't you think it would be well to send some men to raise the carriage at once? It will soon be quite dark."

"You are right, lass. I'll take Brent and two more chaps, and see the job done myself, and drive the horses home. Gib isn't to be trusted. I shouldn't wonder a bit if we found him at th' 'Hare and Hounds.'"

"You had better go into the house and have a wash, Nelson," said Miriam, "your face is streaked with blood, and get some plaster for your head."

An hour later, as Mr. Ruberry drove towards Oaken Cleugh, he met Robin going home.

"Drat the fellow!" he muttered. "He has been a bonnie time getting his head patched. I should have seen him off th' premises before I started; but Miriam's a sensible lass. I'm sure she's to be trusted, whatever Robert says."

END OF VOL. II.

www.ingramcontent.com/pod-product-compliance
Lightning Source LLC
Chambersburg PA
CBHW060552030726
47498CB00005B/1365